MIDNIGHT WHISPERS

P. RAYNE

Cover Designer: Regina Wamba

Line Editor: Joy Editing

Proofreader: My Brother's Editor

About Midnight Whispers

I spend my nights slinging drinks at Black Magic Bar or taking my clothes off at the local strip club. After my father passed, my stepmother gave me no other choice.

But when I break free of the chains binding me to my family estate, I find myself with nowhere to go. Until Nero Voss, the youngest of the billionaire Voss brothers, offers me a room at Midnight Manor. Now, I'm under his watchful gaze and enjoying it more than I should.

I shouldn't give in to temptation, he is my stepsister's ex-fiancé after all, but the pull toward him grows stronger by the day. I fight, but I'm losing the battle.

Nero is keeping secrets, though.

What he doesn't know is that I'm keeping secrets, too.

the Midnight Manor series

MIDNIGHT WHISPERS

P. RAYNE

AUTHOR'S NOTE

Trigger warnings can be found on our website if you want
to check them out.

PLEASE NOTE:
These warnings contain major spoilers.

https://piperrayne.com/midnight-manor

I hate my stepsisters as much as I hate the gray-haired woman in front of me. The only reason I remain in this home is because the estate holds so many happy memories from my childhood with my father and mother, when she was alive. Until Louise sank her claws into my father. This home is the only one I've ever known, and I can't imagine living anywhere else.

The real reason I want to go tonight is because I've never been to a ball. I want to mingle and dance and feel pretty and just be outside of my regular life for a few hours. I don't want to be Cinder who strips at the club and slings drinks at a dive bar only to hand over her money to her stepmom in order to keep the estate going. I want to be the woman I am inside my head. A woman with hopes and dreams, who looks toward the future with excitement and curiosity.

"You expect me to believe that?" Louise scoffs. "You're probably seething with jealousy that she's landed a Voss brother. You don't wish her well any more than I wish you were my biological daughter."

Her words are a slap across the face, and a stark reminder of how alone I am in the world since my father passed.

"I won't be any trouble, I promise." I hate the begging note in my voice, but I'm desperate to have this one night to fuel my dreams for years to come.

"You won't be trouble because you aren't going."

Tears build in the corners of my eyes, although I try with everything in me to not reveal the hurt she causes me. The woman gets off on me begging, and this is the one occasion I'm willing to give her what she wants.

3

"Please, Louise." I put my hands in a prayer pose.

She rolls her eyes. "When was the last time you washed the draperies? If you get it done, and there's time after, you can join us."

My shoulders sag. There's no way all the draperies will fit in our machine at the same time, which means loads of laundry and hours of work.

"I'll never be able to finish in time."

"There're always complaints coming from your mouth. Fine, come then, but I want those draperies done tomorrow before you go work your shift at that deplorable place."

I bolt up. "Oh, thank you so much!" My excitement dies when tendrils of smoke rise up behind her. "What's that?"

"What's what?" She slowly turns toward the ironing board.

I rush around her and gasp. The iron lies flat on the front of my dress, smoke billowing out.

"Oh dear, how'd that happen?" Louise says.

I pull the iron off. The light blue silk is charred. Wetness pools in my eyes, and I whip toward Louise. "It's ruined."

"Such a pity. I guess you won't be joining us after all." She doesn't look at me and leaves the room, her laughter ringing down the hall.

I squeeze my eyes shut, and the tears fall down my cheeks. My chest aches as if a boulder is sitting on it. All I wanted was one night, one night to have fun and feel free. She couldn't even let me have that.

A few minutes later, I cou downstairs. I leave my room and look over the banister at the entry foyer. My stepsisters are talking and laughing, dressed in their gorgeous and expensive dresses, checking their appearances in the ornate mirror. Maude's red hair is pulled back, and she's dressed in a navy blue dress that I could never afford, a silver mask dangling from her hand.

Tonight's event is a masquerade ball the Voss family holds every year to raise funds for charity, though from the rumors I've heard about the Voss family, they have more than enough money to match whatever they raise.

Dru is beside her, her black curls dangling nearly to her waist, wearing a green dress that's equally as gorgeous and expensive as Maude's. She sees me from the corner of her eye and flicks her hand, grabbing Maude's attention.

Maude turns, and her lips form a cunning smile. "Heard about your dress. Too bad."

"Don't act like you care," I say with as much venom as I can muster.

She blinks rapidly and brings her hand to her chest as if I've offended her. "Why, of course I do, sweet sister. Believe me, I'd love nothing more than to have you there witnessing what you'll never have—a rich, successful, handsome man. Bet Tits & Tassels doesn't have a lot of those."

She and Dru bend over laughing. My fists clench on top of the banister. I'm only working at the strip club to be able to meet their financial demands, but they love to shove it in my face as though I choose to dance there. If Louise had let me go to college after high school, I could have worked somewhere else and made as much money as she demanded.

My stepmom walks into the foyer, her heels clicking on the stone. She follows her daughters' gazes up to me. "Don't wait up. Who knows how long we'll be out celebrating."

They all laugh and walk out the door. The bang sounds like a prison cell door, locking me in here.

Instead of sinking to the floor and crying, I return to my room. The only thing worse that could happen would be to accidentally burn down the whole house.

I unplug the iron and stare at my ruined dress, wishing there was some way to salvage it. The burn mark is front and center. An idea comes to me the more I inspect it. If I cut from the burn mark down off of the dress and resew the hem, it might work. The front would show my legs and be way shorter than the back, but that's a dress style. Not what I imagined, but it would still be gorgeous.

Yanking the dress from the ironing board and grabbing my sewing supplies, I get to work. An hour later, the dress is finished and I stare at my reflection, twirling around to check all angles. Damn, I did a good job. Now I just have to drive there and somehow get inside. I'll be late, since I overhead my stepsisters and stepmom talking about taking Nero's private plane, but I can drive fast. I'm sure I was never added to the guest list, but I'm confident I can charm my way into the ball.

One skill I've learned from working at the strip club is how to charm men out of their money. Surely I can sweet-talk my way into a party.

"I need to know what you think of Maude. I'm nervous as hell, and I need to know you have no real objections."

My brother's shoulders relax. "Do whatever you think is right. You're a grown man. Make the decision yourself."

Does Anabelle have some potion she's drugging him with? I'm shocked but pleased.

"I'm going to run to the ladies' room and let you two talk," Anabelle says. "I'll meet you back at the table?"

Asher places a chaste kiss on her lips before his face runs along her cheek to her ear, whispering something that makes her blush. Could he be in love? Asher in love? I never would have thought.

"I promise you this is the right decision." I clamp his shoulder. I'm not sure if I'm trying to convince him or me.

"Do you know how you're going to do it?"

I grin. "I booked a room for us at a nearby hotel. I've arranged for the suite to be filled with flowers and desserts. I'm going to run a bubble bath for us and ask her to marry me."

"You're a regular Prince Charming."

I roll my eyes. Out of my four brothers, I'm the most in tune with my emotions. Maybe because I'm the youngest, and they all protected me. They all have these hard exteriors that I don't, but I know my brothers. When they meet the love of their lives, they'll be running bubble baths and sprinkling rose petals on beds too. "You'd do the same for Anabelle."

He ignores my statement and instead sticks one hand between us and the other clamps onto my shoulder. "Good luck."

"Thanks, big brother. Listen, if you don't mind, I'm going to take off. I just want it over."

"The rest of us will handle things here."

"Awesome." I make my way off the dance floor, but something catches my eye before I do.

Or rather *someone.*

A blonde with her hair pulled back, wearing a light blue dress that shows off an amazing pair of legs, is trying to free herself from a man who's clearly had too much to drink. I don't recognize him, but then again, the masks don't help any. I turn in their direction, walking toward them. The guy pulls her into him.

What the fuck?

I don't want to cause a scene, but this guy needs to keep his hands to himself before I break them. I fucking hate men who are physically aggressive with women. It hits too close to home with how my father treated my mother. I was so young when my mother died, but my most vivid memories are the ones where my father was physically abusive to her.

I walk up to them, not pausing for a beat, and place my hand on the small of her back, standing as close as I can to her. "There you are. Ready for that dance you promised me?" I glare at the man who is twenty or thirty years her senior.

Through her silver mask, her blue eyes widen. I stare into the depths, lost for a moment.

She's much better at recovering herself from whatever just passed between us. "I... yes, yes, sorry I was held up."

The man mumbles something and reluctantly steps back.

"Shall we?" I gesture to the dance floor.

Her eyes scan the area as if she's here with someone else whom she's scared might find her in my arms, but she walks toward the dance floor. She winds around couples dancing until we're cocooned in the middle of the wooden floor. I place my hand around her waist and hold her hand between our bodies. As I guide her around the dance floor, I'm surprised it doesn't feel awkward.

Her perfume of jasmine and sandalwood assaults me as her feet easily move with mine. She's a natural dancer, allowing me to lead effortlessly. I'm distracted by her tits pressing against my chest. Hers are bigger than average, and it's impossible for me not to notice. I shouldn't compare her to Maude, but I can't help it.

"Thank you for saving me. I was trying to be polite, but he wouldn't take no for an answer. Usually I have no trouble dealing with men like him, but he was more persistent than most."

"Happy to help."

Again, she scours the crowd.

"Are you here with anyone?" Not sure where the douchebag of a man she's with that would let her out of his sight for a second, but she's definitely concerned about someone spotting us.

"No, I'm here by myself."

"You're looking everywhere but at me. Figured you were with someone here."

She chuckles, and my stomach swoops from the carefree lilt of her laughter.

"What's your mask?" she asks, changing the subject.

"A raven."

She studies it for a beat. "It's a lot fancier than everyone else's."

"I wear a mask on other occasions, so I invested in a nice one."

"Oh, so you come to this event every year?" Her head tilts, and one of the curls from her updo escapes. I force myself not to tuck it behind her ear.

I smirk. "Something like that."

"Are you here with someone?" she asks.

Her question is innocent enough. I'm currently dancing closely with her. I have the urge not to mention Maude, which is an asshole move, but the thought of telling her I'm here with someone else feels like a blow to the gut.

"I am." I circle her around, knowing I need to be honest. "In fact, I'm proposing to her later this evening."

Her footsteps stumble, and my hand slides down, clasping her waist so she doesn't fall.

"Sorry." She strips her gaze from me, and her body grows tense in my hold.

Maybe I'm not the only one who feels this pull between us. I've only been around this woman for a few minutes, and I don't even know what she looks like without a mask. I need to ignore whatever this is since I'm proposing to another woman tonight.

The song ends and another one starts, but she steps out of my arms.

"Thanks again for the help. Good luck with your proposal. I wish you a lifetime of happiness." She turns toward the crowd.

"Together."

She stops and glances at me over her shoulder. "Sorry?"

"You forgot to add together at the end of your sentence."

For the first time, her smile falters, and her lips thin. "No, I didn't."

As she disappears through the crowd, I realize that I didn't even get her name.

I make my way back to Maude, but the mysterious blonde lingers in the back of my mind. Not the best sign.

CHAPTER
THREE

NERO

APPROXIMATELY ONE YEAR LATER...

I blink at the picture, zooming in to get a closer look.

Still unbelieving, I close the picture to re-read the anonymous email. I had to have missed something.

To: nvoss@vossenterprises.com

From: fairygodmother@email.com

Subject: Something you need to see

I don't like being the bearer of bad news, but you deserve to know.

That's the entire message and accompanying it is the picture. I open it again and am faced with the image of my fucking fiancée naked in the arms of another man in a bed.

The picture has been shot through a window and neither Maude nor the man are aware.

What the fuck?

There's no question Maude has been off lately, but I thought it was the pressure of our wedding this fall and all the planning and decision-making we've had to do. That, coupled with the fact that Asher and Anabelle were married this spring, something she's told me on more than one occasion takes the shine off of our nuptials.

But this... her cheating was not on my radar.

Before I jump to conclusions, I download the photo and check all the metadata. This photo may be old. My hope is dashed when I find it was taken a few days ago. On the night that Maude said she'd be working late and had to do a few wedding prep errands.

"Fuck!" I slam my fist down on my desk.

Did I miss obvious signs all along? Ironically, I never told Maude that I enjoy sharing my partner because I didn't think she'd be into it.

I like sharing.

But I don't like liars.

And I'm certainly not going to marry one.

Our sex has always been... enjoyable, but not earth-shattering. And I was okay with that. I pushed my desires aside because I thought we had something more. I thought Maude loved me for me, not my name, nor my money, but if that's the case, then why is sleeping with another man behind my back?

Putting Maude aside, who the hell sent this to me?

Asher.

My brothers always think they have to protect me like they did when we were younger, but I'm old enough now to take care of myself. They need to learn to stop interfering. I'm half tempted to walk down to my big brother's wing and tell him off.

I look at the picture again. *Maybe I should.*

I print the picture, swipe it off the printer, and stomp toward Asher's office. I don't bother knocking before pushing open the door. Anabelle is in his lap, and I've interrupted something, but I don't give a shit. His scowl doesn't scare me.

"Next time knock," he says.

I temper my anger to address my sister-in-law, since she has no part in our fight. "Anabelle, may I have a word with my brother alone?"

She looks at Asher, back at me, and slides off his lap. "I'll see you in a bit." She squeezes my shoulder when she walks by me, almost in sympathy.

Damn it all to hell. She knows.

The door closes, and Asher's eyes swing to me. "What the hell is your problem?"

I cross the room, slamming the printed picture on top of some papers. "What the fuck is this?"

He looks at it and back at me. "Looks like your fiancée fucking another man."

"Cut the shit. I know you're the one who sent it to me. What's wrong? Didn't have the balls to tell me you'd hired someone to follow her?"

Asher's eyes narrow, and he slowly pushes the picture toward me without his eyes leaving mine. "I didn't. Though it's not because I didn't want to, believe me. I knew she'd screw you over from day one."

"Asher, the all-knowing. How do you know Anabelle won't do the same?"

His jaw clenches, and I'm happy I struck a nerve. "Watch it, that's my wife."

He's right. Anabelle would never do anything to hurt Asher. Their love is true. But I'd thought mine was, too.

"Just admit you're the one who sent me this. You're always interfering and acting like you need to protect all of us, but you go that extra mile for me."

"It seems in this case I was right."

My fists clench, and I take deep breaths not to lunge across the desk. "Just wanted to let you know that your message has been received, and there will be no wedding."

I spin on my heel and cross the room, afraid that if I stick around any longer, we'll come to blows.

"Nero."

I stop but don't turn around.

"I'm sorry."

I open the door and slam it shut behind me. He can shove his sorry up his ass.

The minute I reach my room, I text Maude and tell her I'll meet her at her family estate this evening. She asks if everything is okay, but I don't answer. It will do her good to be anxious about why I might be pissed.

I ARRIVE at Maude's family estate and get out of my car, stretching my fingers to ease the ache from how tightly I was gripping the steering wheel.

I knock on the door, and seconds later, she answers. Her red hair flows down her shoulders. Once I looked at her and felt only love. Now my eyes struggle to stay on her. As I've done all my life, I keep my expression neutral as she ushers me inside.

"How are you?" She leans in for a kiss, and I give her my cheek. She pulls back, her face contorted with confusion. "Is everything okay?"

"Where can we talk?"

Maude studies me and gestures to her left. "The parlor."

Once we're inside, I wait for her to take a seat first and take the one directly across from her. She notices the slight, her body stiffening when I don't sit beside her.

"Nero, what's going on?" She clasps her hands in her lap as though she's some pious woman. What a fucking joke.

"How are you feeling about the wedding?" I ask.

Her shoulders lose some of the tension, easing into the couch cushion. "I'm thrilled. A little stressed about everything being perfect, but I get to marry the love of my life. What isn't there to be excited about?"

A caustic laugh erupts from my throat, and her smile dies. I'm not sure she's ever heard that sound from me—we've rarely gotten into fights since we started dating.

"If I'm the love of your life..." I reach into the inside pocket of my suit, pull out the picture, and unfold it. "Then who is this?" I place it on the table between us.

She glances down, eyes narrowing as if she doesn't recognize herself, the man, or the bed. Finally, her face pales a ghostly white. "I... I..." She looks up from the picture and back down and up again as if she's stalling to make some excuses as to why she's sleeping around. "Where did you get this?"

I arch an eyebrow. "That's the question you're going to ask?"

Her back straightens, her shoulders square, as if she's offended I would bring this to her. "The picture is old." She bolts off the couch, choosing anger over getting caught rather than regret.

A cold smirk forms on my lips. "I looked at the metadata."

Her eyes search, and her body fidgets. "It not true. I swear."

She rushes around the table to sit beside me, taking my hand and clutching it between her modest breasts. It's insulting that she's suggesting someone could pull one over on me. There's a reason I'm in charge of anything to do with computers and digital security for Voss Enterprises. I'm the fucking expert.

"Do you really think I wouldn't look into it? The photo hasn't been tampered with. Neither has the metadata. This was taken the night you told me you were working late and had wedding prep to do. I didn't realize that meant spreading your legs for someone else."

She studies my face and seems to realize she's cornered, but her desperation won't let her give up. She decides to try a different angle. "I can explain. It was a one-time thing. He's—"

I pull my hand from hers and stand, straightening my suit sleeves. "I don't care who he is. He can have you."

Her head rears back, and her mouth hangs open as if I struck her. "What are you saying?"

I lean in over her and meet her gaze. "There's nothing I hate more than a liar."

She reaches for my suit sleeve, her arms wrapping around mine, and stares up at me with pleading eyes. "But I made a mistake. I can make it up to you—"

I'm not interested in watching her beg to keep my affections. "The wedding is off. Keep the ring, I don't give a shit."

She stands, and I step back. "That's it? You're just going to leave me?"

I keep my expression neutral. "What did you expect? It's too bad. If you'd told me you were interested in sleeping with another man, maybe we could have shared you." I shrug. "What's done is done. As are you and I. Goodbye, Maude." I make my way toward the door.

"Wait! Wait! Nero!" She rushes behind me and grips my elbow, trying to turn me around. "I'm sorry."

I face her with one hand on the doorknob of the estate's front door. "I'm sure you are."

I swing the door open and walk toward my car, listening to her dissolve into sobs behind me. When I reach my car, I glance at the front door. Maude's sister comforts her as their mother stands in the open doorway, watching me leave with a pissed-off expression that could challenge mine. Once the door is shut, I start my engine.

Good riddance.

I punch the steering wheel, my emotions coming to the surface once I'm alone.

Taking one last look at an estate I'll never be at again, a flicker of movement in the attic catches my eye, but when I look up, the curtain is in place over the small window. I must be seeing things. No one else lives in that house, and I just saw all three women at the front door.

Shoving the car into drive, I whip around and then down the dirt road that leads out to the main road, ready to put this marriage shit behind me.

Never wanting to talk about that, I instead dare to ask him, "What's your plan for Rapsody?"

He takes a hit and passes the joint back to me. "No plan."

I scoff, take a drag, then toss it on the grass and crush it with the heel of my boot. "Bullshit, brother. You always have a plan."

"Whatever." He picks up the bottle of whiskey and takes a swig.

"I don't know if it's a special forces thing or if it's just you, but you always have a plan. So what is it?"

He's quiet for a minute, but eventually he answers. "I don't know what went down with you and Maude, but if I had to guess, I'd say you might have some idea now how I felt four years ago when Rapsody up and left me."

My jaw clenches, and I put out my hand for him to pass me the bottle.

"So you do have a plan." I tip back the bottle.

"Of course I do."

I chuckle and take another swig.

"I'm going to make her fall for me again. Make her think all is forgiven and that I'm the same man she met back in Atlanta. Show her how wonderful our life together could be. Ruin her, in all the ways that count, and leave her the same way she did me."

I pass the bottle back to him, and he sets it in the grass.

"You think you can do that without falling for her?" I ask.

"Of course I can." He glares at me.

He's lying to himself. "She's the only woman I've ever seen you give a shit about. More than that—you were going to marry her, Kol. You've never even bothered to really date anyone before her. You fuck them for a bit and then move on, never even talk about the women with any of us."

"We can't all be Prince Charming, kid." He ruffles my hair like he used to when we were younger. It pisses me off now just as much as it did then.

"Fuck off." I shove his hand away. "And nice try distracting me, but it's not gonna work."

"I made the mistake of falling for her once. I won't do it again." His voice is hard.

I shake my head and fall back in the grass. "For the record, I think your plan is shit."

"I didn't ask for your fucking opinion."

I stare at the sky as the sun slips behind a cloud, and my high kicks in, keeping my thoughts and my limbs nice and fuzzy feeling. Neither of us speaks for a time until the words I often wonder about press against my lips, pushing themselves out.

"Do you think we're cursed?" I ask.

"What do you mean?"

I prop myself up on my elbows. "This family. This manor. Do you think it's cursed, and that's why we've gone through all the shit we have, or do you think it's karma for all the bad shit or something?"

Kol pulls at a blade of grass. "Most people would say we're lucky to have been born into a billionaire's family."

I give him a cutting look. "They obviously didn't know our father."

Mentioning him brings back the stark reminder of what went down the day he died all those years ago. From the look on Kol's face, I'm guessing it's the same for him.

"I think some people are just evil, and we happened to be the sons of one of those people. But then we had Mom, and she was... she was everything." He reaches for the whiskey and slugs back another mouthful. "Maybe karma is what balances the scales. We had Mom, and we were born into money, so it gave us Dad. I dunno." He passes me the bottle, and I sit up to drink some, then wipe my mouth with the back of my hand.

Internally, I chuckle. If only dear old dad could see me now. I'd have a black eye from being so improper as to wipe my mouth with the back of my hand. Bastard.

"What happened that day—"

His head whips in my direction. "We agreed not to talk about it. Ever." He narrows his eyes.

I look away from him, knowing he's right and also knowing it's for the best. Then I spot Rapsody standing in the distance, and I smirk. "Hey, Rapsody," I call, waving. "Why don't you join us?"

Kol stiffens and looks at me as though he'd like to slit my throat.

She hesitates, holding a small canvas and paint. But she sits beside me, which I'm sure will piss off my brother, arranging her dress so the fabric covers her bare legs.

I eye the paints. "You're a painter?"

Her cheeks pinken. "I don't know if I'd call myself a painter, but I enjoy it. I find it relaxing. Helps to clear my head."

Kol scoffs.

"What?" she snipes, her voice full of attitude. Who would have thought she had it in her to challenge my brother? She's so sweet and innocent.

"Own it. You're a talented painter," Kol says.

Her forehead creases. "How would you know?"

"I was in the conservatory this morning and saw your paintings."

I laugh and shake my head. "I love being right."

Rapsody turns to me. "What do you mean?"

"Ignore him. He's drunk. And high," Kol says.

Her eyes focus on the bottle of booze in the grass. "Are you guys celebrating something?"

A caustic laugh leaves my mouth. "Certainly not. It's a shit day for us Vosses, second only to the day that our mother was murdered. And today..." I lean in and look her in the eye. "Today is especially shitty for me."

"What happened?" Sweet thing. She appears genuinely concerned.

much I enjoyed dancing and performing. Up until my dad died, I'd taken dance classes and competed. But with his passing, all that ended abruptly.

Being allowed out of the house to build relationships was the first positive. But when I got promoted from cocktail waitress to dancer and was able to dance on stage, seeing the way the men responded... a little spark of joy lit in the darkness. My confidence that Louise and her daughters had run through the mud sprouted inside me. And I needed it after years of them tearing down my self-worth.

When they make comments about working at T&T's, I pretend I'm ashamed because if Louise found out that I like working there, she'd put a stop to it.

"It's not that." I bow my head. "If I'm late, they might fire me. But it will all be done before you wake up in the morning."

I grab the tea towel, dry the pan quickly, and put it away in the cupboard. Then I race upstairs to grab their laundry and get it in the machine before I leave. I'll have to throw it in the dryer and stay up to fold it when I return in the middle of the night.

Once it's in the machine, I trudge up to my attic bedroom with all my worn and dated furniture and draperies. Each piece deemed too old or ugly to be elsewhere on the estate. But it's the one place in this house that's mine.

I riffle through the bits of fabric that make up most of my work costumes and decide on a bright blue slingshot thong suit, quickly sliding it on. Normally I'd change there, but since I'm running late, I'll have little to no time to get ready there. Then I slide on a T-shirt and jean shorts over top and quickly brush my hair.

Thankfully, the stage makeup will cover my tiredness. Racing through the house, I don't bother to say goodbye before I leave through the front door, jumping into my blue Toyota. My engine sputters as I head down the drive.

I make it to T&T's in record time, and Aiyden, the bouncer, holds open the back door for me. He's a sweetheart of a man to all the dancers and protects us from sleazebags who act as if they have some right to our bodies.

"Thanks, Aiyden."

The burly man dressed in black smiles. "Better hurry."

"Cin, you're almost late!" Trina shouts from where she's helping another dancer pull up her fishnet outfit without ripping it.

"I'm sorry. I'll be ready."

Trina danced for decades and recently aged out. Now she's kind of like our house mom. She gets paid to keep the dancers in line and make sure things run smoothly in the back of the house.

I yank off my T-shirt and shorts, grabbing my heels from my bag. Lisa, another dancer, comes off stage, and I head over to her.

"How is it out there tonight?"

She frowns. "Not as busy as we'd like."

Another shitty night? It's been a pretty regular occurrence, which is why I took a second job bartending at Black Magic

Bar. What I brought home from the strip club wasn't enough for Louise. Online porn and a crappy economy have reduced the number of people who come out to see live dancers.

"I didn't catch you before you left last night." I hand a wad of bills to her.

Lisa recently left her abusive boyfriend, two small kids in tow, and has been hiding out in a shitty motel room the next county over. I overheard her telling one of the other girls that she only had enough for another week and no place to go.

"Cin, I can't take this from you." She pushes the cash back in my direction, but I shake my head and hold up my hands.

"Yes, you can. It will help you stay for another few nights."

Her eyes grow glossy, and she pulls me in for a hug. Her costume's sequins poke my skin. "Thank you so much. I won't forget it."

"It's nothing. I don't want you to go back to that asshole."

She gives me a watery smile and nods. "You let me know if you ever need anything."

"I will. I have to go do my makeup, or Trina's going to have my ass." I wink, and she laughs.

I plop down in front of my station and quickly put on my stage makeup—heavy silvery eyeshadow with dark fake eyelashes and severe black cat eye eyeliner, a heavy lip, and pink blush with a lot of highlighter to reflect the lights on stage. I run a brush through my hair again, wishing I had a few extra dollars this week to get it trimmed, but it's worth going without so that Lisa and her kids stay safe.

As I set down my brush, Trina calls, "Cin, you're up!"

I toss my belongings into my locker and rush through the change room past the other girls and over to the side stage, waiting to hear my intro. I'll dance to one song on stage, then work the room for the second song, then return to the stage for the last one. After that, I'll cool down, then go out to work the floor for lap dances or private shows in the VIP area. Then I'll be back on stage a few hours later. My bones ache just thinking about the night ahead of me.

A slowed-down, reverb version of "Where Have You Been" plays, and the announcer starts my intro. I wait behind the stage, shaking out my arms to dissipate my nerves.

"Ladies and gentlemen, prepare yourself for a tantalizing experience like no other as we welcome to the stage the embodiment of sensuality, the mesmerizing enchantress, the one and only, Cin!"

I rush the few stairs to the stage. The crowd claps and cheers, but it's not nearly as loud as it used to be. I've danced here long enough to tell how many people are in the room just from the amount of applause. It's going to be another hard night to earn enough tips to satisfy Louise plus have enough left over for me.

Walking down the runway, I accentuate the pivot of my hips and make eye contact with the men sitting in the front row. They'll be the ones who will fork out the cash tonight.

I grab the pole with one hand and twirl around, spreading my legs to tease the men. The pole rests between my ass cheeks when I bend over to touch my ankles, so they imagine it's their dick resting in the same spot.

When the bass kicks in on the chorus, I grab the pole with two hands and gyrate my hips with the music, smiling at the sea of men's faces to judge who is the most interested so I can pay them special attention when I finish my set and head to the floor.

I stretch against the pole and pop down with my legs spread, crawling toward the man waving money. The lust in his eyes sends a surge of confidence through me, as does the knowledge that the men behind me are checking out my ass in this thong. When I reach the edge of the stage, I sit up and arch my chest toward him so that he can place the money between one of the strings of my outfit and my skin. He licks his lips, and I move on to the next man, crawling across the stage.

A tingling sensation roves over my body, a sense of someone watching me. With a sultry expression, I toss my hair over my shoulder and glance behind me. A man is sitting in a booth in the back corner, but he's shrouded in shadows so I can't see his face. I turn back to the men around the stage, but I can't stop feeling him watch me collect money from the other men.

"Drive You Insane" comes on, and I make my way off the stage to work the crowd, grinding on men's laps, teasing them, leaning in and presenting them with my cleavage that's barely covered by the blue fabric. Most of the men are regulars and have already been warned about touching. The only touching that's allowed is in the VIP area where you pay to play.

My attention flickers to the man in the back corner, trying to make him out. Although I can't see him, I can *feel* him watching me, and for some reason, it's turning me on.

By the time I've made my way almost around the entire room, the song changes to "Naughty Girl" by Beyoncé and I climb up on stage to remove the minimal clothing I'm wearing.

I used to remove my top in the first minute of the first song, but Trina taught me that it's all about making them want it and not giving it to them right away. That's what gets the dollars pried out of their sweaty palms and gets you an invite into the VIP room where you make real money.

I spin around the pole in a brass monkey, and my blonde hair sweeps across the floor. Then I do a few more moves before standing and hinting at removing the fabric over my breasts by tugging on the strings and holding them up. The men cheer, clapping to egg me on, and after teasing them a few more times, I slowly pull the straps down to reveal myself. They cheer, throw some money on stage, and I crawl over to collect it, stuffing it in my thong.

We're not allowed to take our bottoms off—at least not in the front of the house.

When the song ends, I take the rest of my money and climb off stage. Before I step down the stairs, I take one last glance in the corner, wondering who the mystery man is.

CHAPTER
SIX

NERO

I end up passing out in bed, but when I wake, the idea to go to T&T's is still fresh in my mind, so I recruit Damien to drive me, knowing I'm nowhere near sober yet.

He drops me at the entrance of T&T's, and I lean my head back in the car before he pulls away. "Just park it. I'll find you when I'm done."

"Yes, sir." He nods.

I hope Damien didn't have plans tonight, although he probably did. None of us use him to drive us at night much anymore unless it's a special occasion. But I'm not in any condition to drive.

I slip the bouncer a hundred-dollar bill and point at the booth in the back, opting to sit away from everyone in case someone recognizes me. My older brothers garner more attention in the press, but since my engagement became public knowledge, I've been in the gossip rags more than usual. Can't wait to see what happens when they find out my fiancée is a lying bitch and there isn't a wedding.

I slide into the booth, and the waitress dressed in a silver triangle bikini top and black booty shorts comes over. She has a small rack, which doesn't do much for me, but she's cute. After she returns with my drink, I shift my attention to the stage as the DJ gets set to announce the next dancer.

"Ladies and gentlemen, prepare yourself for a tantalizing experience like no other as we welcome to the stage the embodiment of sensuality, the mesmerizing enchantress, the one and only, Cin!"

The dancer walks out, and my drink is poised at my lips, but I immediately set it back down on the table because holy shit, this woman deserves all my attention. Her long blonde hair sways as she makes her way down the stage, sashaying with a sultry and confident look in her eye, almost as if she enjoys performing.

From what I remember, dancers look as though they're going through the motions, or their eyes are glassy with the telltale signs that they've been dabbling beforehand, probably to get through the night. But not this woman.

I appreciate all women, but everyone has their preferences. And this woman is built as if she popped out of my fantasies. Voluptuous. She has big natural tits, and my palms itch to feel the weight of them. Her waist nips in, then her shapely hips curve out.

The little blue number she's wearing doesn't leave much to the imagination, but it's still not enough. I'm eager to see her take off the rest of her clothes.

I'm granted a good view of her plump ass when she crawls across the stage, and even though I should have whiskey dick with the amount I've drunk today, my cock twitches when I imagine her bent over in front of me in that exact position.

Almost as though she can sense my thoughts, she looks back over her shoulder at my table.

She continues her performance, and when the song changes, she comes down off the stage to work the crowd. The men are practically salivating as she approaches them, and I have no doubt one or more of them will probably invite her into a VIP room at some point.

Damn, I wish I could watch that go down.

I slide my hand down and adjust myself.

The third song comes on, and she returns to the stage, using the pole to show us how flexible she is, collecting more money from the men in the front row. The song ends way too soon, and she's gone.

I watch the next dancer, but my interest is lost quickly. Images of Cin ping-pong in my head. I toss back my drink then pull cash from my wallet and drop it on the table before getting up and making my way to the exit.

When I get into the back of the car, Damien looks at me in the rearview mirror. "That was quick."

"Saw what I needed."

He starts the car. "Headed back to the manor?"

I shake my head. "No, we're gonna stay here for a while."

That buzz of adrenaline in my veins that was once so familiar returns. Probably not a good sign, but I don't have it in me to care. For the first time in the past week, I'm not moping around, fixating on how Maude got one over on me.

No, now I have something—or someone—new to fixate on. As long as I don't take it too far, it won't be a problem.

WEEKS LATER, I ease my car through Magnolia Bend but slam on the brakes after I pass Black Magic Bar. The same Toyota that Cin drives is parked in the side lot of the dive bar. I shouldn't know what car she drives, but I've become a regular at T&T's since the first night I saw her. Not that she's aware. I sit in the back booth and only stay long enough to watch her performance, then I wait patiently out in the parking lot to watch her leave.

I consider it a point of pride that I haven't followed her home or looked her up online. It means I have boundaries, which I didn't always have.

After I reverse my car, I park it in the side lot and make my way up to the front porch of the bar, stand to the side of one of the windows, and peek inside. Cin is behind the bar, chatting with a guy seated along the bar. She bartends here too?

The stripper gig doesn't earn enough for her then.

Surprised, I make my way back to my car and ease it out of the parking lot, finding a parking spot farther down the street where I can see the front of the bar.

Some time passes, and I spot Anabelle and Rapsody leaving Scuttlebutt Salon. It takes me a minute to recognize Rapsody because she's cut off all her long hair. They don't notice me and venture down the sidewalk before going into Black Magic Bar.

A while later, Kol's car drives down Main Street. I duck down in my seat, hoping he doesn't notice me. He must not because when I look, he's opening the door of the bar and going inside.

Something must go down because Anabelle leaves with a concerned look on her face about a minute later. A short while after that, Kol tugs Rapsody out of there.

He's up shit creek with that one. He can't control his emotions for her any more than he can control the weather. But Kol will say he can.

I remain on watch until several hours later when Cin leaves the bar and drives out of the parking lot. This time, I follow her. But she doesn't go home. Instead, she drives directly to T&T's.

I park in the front lot, and I wonder if it's finally time to introduce myself to Cin.

CHAPTER
SEVEN

CINDER

When I leave Black Magic Bar and check my phone, there's a flurry of texts from Louise and my stepsisters with a list of chores they want done at the house. I bite back my curse. They're the ones who said I wasn't making enough and the reason I had to take on a second job. Exactly when did they think I'd have time to be their cook and housekeeper too?

Fatigue weighs in my bones as if I'm not in my twenties but rather my eighties. The schedule I keep these days is taking its toll.

"Hey, girl. You ready to do this tonight?" Trina asks when I walk in through the back door.

I paste on a smile. "You know it."

She frowns, sensing something's off, and pushes past some of the other girls getting ready to come over to me. "What's wrong, sweetie?" Her bright pink lipstick is migrating from her lips up into the wrinkles around her upper lip.

"Just tired, that's all." I open my locker and place my purse and bag inside, then spin around to face her.

She squeezes my shoulder. "You need a pick-me-up? Pick your poison."

I have my choice of alcohol, drugs, or even just some energy drinks. It's not a well-guarded secret that a lot of the girls need to be half out of their minds to get on stage. I've always stayed away from that stuff, though, since I've seen enough of the women fall on the slippery slope.

"I'm okay. I'll snap out of it."

She nods. "All right, sweetie. Wear one of your favorite outfits, get your makeup on, curl your hair, and you'll feel better."

She's not wrong. Once I'm done up in my role as an exotic dancer, it boosts my self-confidence. I brought two outfits tonight: one for the stage and one for when I work the room.

Lisa arrives a few minutes after I do. Our schedules have been opposite since last week.

"Lisa, how are things?" I ask when she rushes over to her locker.

"Good, I'm just running behind. My sister was late showing up to watch my kids. Trina's gonna kill me if I'm not ready for my performance."

I step over to my locker and pull out of my purse the cash

that I set aside for her. "You have time. Just hustle. Before I forget, this is for you."

She looks at the money in my hand. "I can't keep taking money from you, Cin."

"Please just take it. I want to help."

Her brow furrows, and she looks as though she wants to say no, but we both know that she won't. She needs the money.

"Thank you." She takes the cash from me and stuffs it into her locker. "I swear I'll pay you back someday."

I shake my head. "I don't want you to. I just want to help you and your kids. Honestly."

She hugs me, squeezing tightly. "Thank you."

The small show of affection leaves me with glossy eyes and a tight throat because I'm so unaccustomed to it. "You're welcome."

I sit in front of one of the mirrors to get ready. Once my hair is curled and placed up in a high ponytail, I do my makeup, then slip into the white thong and sheer halter with rhinestones. I step into my heels and wait for my turn side stage.

Trina is watching from the side of the stage. "Your man's here." She grins.

Though I know who she's talking about, I pretend otherwise. "I don't have a man, Trina."

She rolls her eyes. "That man sits in the same seat every night you perform, and he leaves straight after. He's only here for you, which makes him your man."

I want to insist she's wrong, but the DJ starts with my introduction.

"Ladies and gentleman, get ready to be captivated with every sway of her hips and bounce of her tits. Up next, we have the electrifying Cin!"

The crowd cat-whistles as I step up the few stairs and out onto the stage. Tonight, I'm doing a set with a little more energy, so "Kickstart my Heart" by Motley Crue plays, and I start on the pole with a more aerobic routine.

One glance at the back booth tells me "my man" is indeed shrouded in the shadows. I can't help but look at his figure as I move off the pole and pay attention to the men front and center.

When "Cherry Pie" by Warrant starts, I move to the floor, rubbing myself on anyone who's willing and has cash in hand. I come across more than one erection pressed against my ass, but they do nothing for me. Still, I play along to siphon more cash from them. All the while I'm more than aware of having *his* eyes on me.

Finally, when "Pour Some Sugar on Me" by Def Leppard starts, I climb up on the stage to slow my routine down and tease the men by slowly revealing my top. My performance goes well, and I leave the stage with a stack of cash. Still, it's not enough for what I need, which means I'm going to have to work hard to get some lap dances or get someone back into the VIP room.

"Good show," Trina says as I pass her while coming down the stairs.

I smile at Lisa, who's waiting to do her routine, and I head off in search of some water and a towel to dry the sweat off my body.

Ten minutes later, I've changed into my second outfit—a schoolgirl costume complete with a plaid tie that matches the too-short skirt revealing a black thong under. I'm just hiking the black stockings up to mid-thigh when Trina approaches with a wide smile.

"Your presence has been requested in VIP room number one." Her eyes glitter with excitement.

My head rocks back. "Really? One of the regulars?"

It's unusual to score a VIP room before I've left backstage.

She shrugs. "Not sure. Eric just came and told me. Said he'd be waiting there."

Eric is one of the bouncers who works the VIP rooms and stays outside in the hallway in case any trouble goes down. Patrons have to make arrangements with him to have a dancer join them in a room.

"I'm on it." I check my hair and makeup one last time, then give my boobs a hike up in the tiny black sports bra I'm wearing under the tie before making my way out of the dressing area.

"Remember," Trina says before I pass by. "When their dick is hard, their brain is soft. Go get that money, honey."

I laugh and make my way out. My eyes have to adjust to the lights in the club once I'm in the front of the house since it's dim here with lots of neon signs throughout the space.

A quick glance at the booth in the back tells me that the mystery man is gone. I curb my disappointment. Maybe one of these days he'll stick around, and I'll get to see who he is.

"Room number one?" I ask Eric as I pass him.

He nods. "I think you can fleece him for a lot."

I stop and turn to face him. "What makes you say that?"

"You'll see." He smirks and winks.

Curiosity piqued, I twist the doorknob and push open the door, coming to an abrupt stop.

It's the mystery man. I'm not sure how I exactly know it's him, but I do.

Worse yet, it turns out my mystery man is Nero, my stepsister's ex-fiancé. Interesting that he comes here and watches me every night. Memories of the dance we shared, the feel of his hand on the small of my back. God, his smile. His amazing, sweet smile that Maude was so undeserving of. And now he's here.

His ice-blue eyes bore into me as I take in his clean-shaven face, full lips, and straight nose. This guy could be straight off a runway with his perfectly tousled brown hair and his expensive dress pants and button-down shirt. Designer for sure. I'd know that even if I didn't know that Nero Voss is a billionaire.

It's clear why Eric made the comment he did. Nero isn't wearing the usual jeans and T-shirt most of the guys who come in here do, nor does he exude the energy of a down-home local boy. No, his presence demands your attention, and the way he's looking at me makes me want to preen under his watchful gaze. It reminds me of the night I first saw him at the ball.

He might remember me from the ball, but I'm certain he won't recognize me as Maude's stepsister. I was always forced to hide in the attic whenever he was at the estate. Knowing Maude, she probably never even mentioned that I existed.

"Hi." I turn and close the door behind me.

A sharp intake of breath rushes from him, and when I turn to face him again, it's obvious he was checking out my ass. Or what you can see of it with this short skirt.

With my left hand, I flick the light switch that turns on the neon light, and the room is bathed in red. Then I sashay over and take a seat next to him.

"I'm Cin," I say, though I'm fairly sure he already knows that from watching me dance so many times.

He nods. "Nero."

I smile with flirtation. "Nice to meet you, Nero."

He returns my smile, and my heart rate picks up.

How the hell did Maude ever land this man? She's a grade-A bitch and a horrible person. But she's also a chameleon, so I'm sure she fooled him—for a while at least.

I've never been jealous of Maude for a minute in my life, even though she got all the freedom, all the praise, and all the love. I always knew what kind of person she was, and since I never wanted to be like her, I considered myself lucky, even given my circumstances. But looking at this man and knowing she was able to make him love her, sleep with her... my stomach rots with acid.

"What would you like tonight?"

"How about a lap dance?" He drags a finger from my shoulder down to my elbow. It's a simple move, somewhat innocent even, but I clench my thighs together from the current of electricity concentrating there.

I lean in, and his gaze flicks to my cleavage like most men. "*Just* a lap dance?" I arch an eyebrow.

"Let's start there."

"Fair enough. One song will cost you a hundred dollars." It's more than I can usually get out of any of the guys around this place, but Nero can afford it.

"I'll give you two thousand dollars for the next hour of your time, how does that sound?"

I try not to act as if he's surprised me, but I'm not sure I succeed based on the way one corner of his lips tip up.

"Sounds like we should get started." I stand from the couch and walk over to the wall to turn up the volume of the music.

The music in the VIP rooms is different from what plays in the main club. It's a rotation of sultry music that plays on repeat.

As I make my way back to him, I exaggerate my hip movements and walk to the beat of the music, coming to stand in front of him. He's relaxed, arms splayed across the back of the couch. The muscles in his arms stretch the fabric of his shirt. His blue eyes watch me with intensity, and I turn around and give him my back.

Something about this man rocks me and makes me forget about all my problems outside of this room.

I bend forward, grabbing my ankles and wiggling my ass side to side, staring at him through my legs. He licks his bottom lip, and his eyelids grow heavy with lust. Not wanting to lose any of his attention, I slide back up and set myself in his lap.

A moan escapes me when my weight settles on his hard cock. His *huge* hard cock. He must know I like the feel of it because he raises his hips, pressing into my ass. I slide along his body, gyrating my hips to the beat of the music, and eventually slide the tiny black sports bra up over my head.

"Leave the tie on."

His tone brooks no argument, and my nipples tighten. Tossing the fabric aside, I lean back so his chest is pressed against my back and grind on him. I feel like a cat in heat, as if I'm doing this for my pleasure and not his. If it weren't for the persistent erection pressing into my ass, I might wonder whether I was the only one enjoying this dance because not once have his hands ventured to touch me. I'd be a liar if I said I didn't wish he'd try to cop a feel.

I lean forward and place my hands on his hard thighs, grinding down on his lap and swinging my ponytail from side to side.

Tired of teasing myself, I eventually stand, turn around, and straddle his lap.

Big mistake. Now I see the way he's looking at me as though he's a minute away from devouring me. I grow wetter. I circle my hips on him then raise myself on my knees a bit so that my breasts are in his face, my nipples turgid and begging for attention. They're aching for him to touch, to lick, to play.

I gently move them back and forth over the seam of his lips, acting like a desperate cat.

God, I'd do just about anything for him to open his mouth and wrap his lips around my nipple. They're so hard it's almost painful.

But he doesn't. Instead, he stays in the same position with his arms splayed and watches me intently.

I want to beg him to do it. Do something, anything. Touch me, fondle me, fuck me. *Something.*

I'm not a virgin, and I'm no angel, that's for sure. I've fooled around with men in the VIP rooms before, but I don't cross the line of getting paid to do so. Men can pay for me to dance for them, and I'll shove my naked tits in their face, but I've never accepted money for sexual favors, though I don't judge the girls who do. We're all just doing our best and doing whatever it takes to survive.

I'm only physical with a man because I find him attractive and because I want to mess around with him. I know I'm looking for affection in all the wrong places—case in point, none of these men have ever even bothered to give me an orgasm. It's all about their pleasure when they're in here. But for just a moment, I can pretend I'm in a loving relationship, that someone desires and needs me, no matter how hollow I'm going to feel afterward.

I stand and turn around again, arching my ass out and easing myself across his lap.

When I lean back against him, he nuzzles his head into the crook of my neck and whispers, "Hook your legs on the outside of mine."

His voice is a rough rumble in my ear. It's what I assume is a bedroom voice. The kind that makes you want him to spit out a string of dirty words.

I do as he asks even though it'll be much harder for me to move this way.

"Now touch yourself, princess." I startle, stilling, and he bites my earlobe. "Come on now, be a good princess and touch yourself. We're going to make you come."

It's the "we" part of that statement that gets me to comply.

I bring my hand between my legs and center my fingers over my G-string where my clit is, sucking in a breath when I make contact.

Seconds later, his big warm hand covers mine. The pressure is light at first as he moves my fingers in a circular motion. When he increases the pressure, I tense, my legs automatically trying to close, but he stretches his legs, not allowing me to.

Gradually, he increases the pressure and the pace. My breasts rock as I thrust my hips into our hands. Unable to take the ache, I bring my free hand up and cup my breast. Nero growls in my ear, and I feel the rumble in his chest behind me as I tweak my nipple.

Then his hips thrust up underneath me as though he's fucking me while his hand forces mine to rub my clit faster. My body grows more and more tense, and my legs strain against his, wanting to close, but he refuses to allow it. With my heart beating like a war drum, my body tingles, and the sensation grows stronger, unstoppable.

"I'm going to come."

"That's my girl," he says into my ear.

And even though I'm not his girl and never will be, those three words send me over the edge. I cry out, jerking in his lap as my orgasm washes over me.

He keeps moving his hand over mine, slowing the pace and the pressure until he stops altogether and pulls it away. I want to cry out for him to return his hand to where it was, but I'm still catching my breath and trying to make sense of what happened. I just let my stepsister's ex-fiancé give me the best orgasm ever.

The worst part is, I don't feel bad about it. No, everything about what happened feels oddly right, and I don't know what to do with that realization.

CHAPTER
EIGHT

NERO

I grip Cin by the waist and set her to the side of me, then stand. Reaching into my pocket, I pull out my wallet and drop a wad of cash onto the table, then I adjust my rock-hard cock with a grimace. It's so in need of relief that it's painful.

"Thanks for the lap dance." Without waiting for her to respond or looking at her, I make my way to the door and walk down the hallway.

I had to get out of there because what just happened is only going to fuel my obsession with her. And that's not good. I'm already stalking most of her movements. I can't afford for this to become more than it already is.

I promised my brothers in high school that I wouldn't go there again. The last thing I need to do is give them an excuse to think they need to coddle me.

Shaking the memory from my head, I push out the main door of the club and suck in a breath of fresh air once I'm outside.

Jesus fuck, that woman is phenomenal. Perfect in every way.

"Get your shit together, man." I stalk over to my vehicle, get inside, and peel out of the parking lot.

I drive around with all the windows down, hoping to clear my head, but it doesn't help. Visions of Cin swim in front of me, superimposed over the road in front of me. Knowing nothing is going to help satisfy me except maybe coming into my fist with her name on my lips, I return to Midnight Manor.

A minute after I drive past the iron gates, my phone buzzes with a text from Asher. I hit the button on the screen of my car to have Bluetooth read it to me over the speakers.

"Come to my office. Now."

I roll my eyes, knowing he likely instructed security to tell him when I was back on the property. What the hell could this be about? I've been slacking where work is concerned because I've been watching Cin, but Asher doesn't know that. And if he does, he probably chalks it up to me calling off the wedding and the picture of Maude with another man.

I park my car and pocket the keys, blowing out a breath as I approach the doors of the manor, giving a quick glance at the gargoyles on top. They've given me the creeps since I was a kid.

I make my way to the west wing, where Asher's office is located, and when I arrive, he and Sid are there. Asher's dressed casually in lounge pants and a T-shirt, so he's obviously been spending the night with Anabelle, but Sid's still in a suit—no surprise. He probably sleeps in the damn thing.

"What's this about?" I step over to the living area in his office where they're both seated.

"Have a seat, kid," Sid says.

I clench my jaw to keep from lashing out at the moniker. He only uses it because he knows I've hated it since we were young. It's not as though I'm decades younger than either of them.

Instead of telling Sid where to shove it, I sit in the chair off to the side. "There, I'm sitting. Where's Kol? Usually these ambushes involve all three of you."

"Don't know," Asher says. "Probably has his hands full with Rapsody, if I had to guess. He didn't answer my texts."

"Well, let's get this over with." I wave toward myself.

Asher heaves out a sigh, and Sid leans back into the couch, crossing his legs and splaying one arm out across the back cushions.

"Something concerning has been brought to my attention." Asher lets his statement hang there as if he's expecting me to fill in the blank.

I look between him and Sid. "Enough with the fucking suspense. Just say it." I narrow my eyes, knowing that whatever is going to come out of his mouth, I'm not going to like.

"Are you stalking someone again?" It's easy to see why Sid's the lawyer in the family—he's always so direct.

"Why would you think that?" My question probably raises a red flag.

"It's true then?" Asher arches an eyebrow.

"I'm not stalking anyone." I stand from the chair.

"This is how it started last time," Asher says and stands, too. Sid follows suit. "Something tragic happened in your life and instead of dealing with it, you fixated on—"

"I know how it all went down, okay? I don't need a play-by-play from you."

Sid steps forward and places a hand on my shoulder. "We're just concerned, that's all. We want to make sure you're not too messed up in the head after what happened with Maude."

I push his hand off my shoulder. "That's rich coming from you."

Sid narrows his dark eyes, and I see a glimpse of what lies under the calm and collected façade.

"Enough," Asher snaps. "If you're not stalking someone, where have you been going when you leave here?"

"I didn't realize I had to sign myself out." I cross my arms.

"What were you doing parked downtown? You never go downtown. None of us do," Sid says.

"Don't treat me like you're cross-examining me on the stand, asshole."

"Answer the question," he says.

"All right, fine. You wanna know?" I throw my arms up at my sides. "I've been down at T&T's watching a dancer. Got a lap dance from her tonight and made her come with my hand. Is that enough information?"

Asher and Sid exchange a glance.

"What's her name?" Asher asks.

I shrug. "What's it matter?" He continues to stare at me, and I roll my eyes. "Cin."

Asher blinks rapidly, and his head rocks back.

"Her real name, not her stage name," Sid says.

"I don't know. Like I said... I'm. Not. Stalking. Her."

"You're telling me you haven't done a deep dive on her?" Asher arches an eyebrow.

"I haven't. Like I said. I have it under control."

They both give me a skeptical look, so I turn around and leave the office.

"Make sure it stays that way," Asher calls out, always needing to have the last word.

I stalk back to my room, irritated beyond measure even though I understand why they'd check in. But how did they know in the first place? Obviously, someone saw my car parked downtown. I'm going to have to be more discreet in the future because there's no doubt that I'm not done with Cin. I won't make the mistake of getting as close to her again as I did tonight, but I'll continue to watch from afar until my fascination with her wanes and I'm able to move on.

When I reach my bedroom in the south wing, I go straight to the en suite and strip out of my clothes, then I turn on the shower. Once the water is warm enough, I step into the large walk-in shower and get under the spray.

The hot water works to ease the tension in my body, but it doesn't make any inroads into my mind, where visions of Cin still coast through my brain.

My semi-hard cock rests against my thigh, and I tug on it, remembering the way Cin stole my breath when she first walked into the VIP room and I saw her close up. Those big blue eyes tugged on something in my subconscious, almost as though I knew them from somewhere.

I remember the sultry note in her voice and strengthen my grip, jerking harder. Remembering her heavy tits in my face, I squeeze my balls with my free hand. My head tilts back, and my eyes drift closed. I wanted so badly to bite one of her nipples. Somehow, I stopped myself, knowing that one taste of her skin would never be enough.

When she turned back around and ground down on my cock, I almost came in my pants like a fucking teenage boy. Looking over her shoulder at her swaying tits and her touching herself, I couldn't help but press my hand over hers. But there was no way I could touch her myself. The scent of her on my fingers would drive me to distraction for weeks. Either that or send me careening into full-blown obsession.

I jerk harder on my cock and squeeze my balls again, imagining what she might smell like, taste like. I keep jerking, pretending it's her hand and that she's looking at me with that determined confidence she has when she's performing on stage. Tingling starts at the base of my spine.

Finally, I imagine another man behind her, fondling her tits while she pleasures me, and my load explodes out of me, hitting the shower floor and washing down the drain with any hopes of that image ever coming true.

If I thought this was going to make me feel better, I was wrong. Somehow, I feel even more fucked up than before.

CHAPTER

NINE

NERO

FOUR MONTHS LATER...

In the months since Cin gave me a lap dance, my obsession with her hasn't stopped. I visit T&T's regularly, watching from the booth in the back, but I've somehow managed not to request another lap dance from her, and by the time she comes down to work the crowd, I'm already gone.

I still watch her work at Black Magic Bar, but now instead of parking on the street, I've rented the space above the dog groomer's directly across from the bar. The window gives me the perfect bird's-eye view through the bar window. Though I can't see everything, she's visible when she makes her way to the far end of the bar. It's sad how much I live for those fleeting glimpses of her.

It's not a problem, though. It's gone no further than that. I don't know where she lives. I haven't hacked into her life online. I've remained under control.

At least that's what I tell myself when I'm gazing out the window on New Year's Eve, waiting for Cin to finish her shift at the bar and wondering if she's heading to T&T's after.

I'm going to be late for dinner at the manor. Anabelle and Rapsody insisted on us eating together before we go our separate ways to ring in the new year. I have to choose to either abandon my post or stick it out and piss off my family. My laugh echoes through the empty room. It's not really a choice.

When Cin makes an appearance at the end of the bar, I lean forward in my seat. Her back is to me, and I see her fingers fly over the screen of her phone, texting so fast I assume she's agitated by someone. She shoves her phone in the back pocket of her jeans, and when she turns around to face the bar again, there's a stricken look on her face. Someone has pissed her off.

My chest tightens with the need to remove that person from her life. She shouldn't ever have to deal with assholes —I'll do that for her. But I don't need to know more about her life. I can't even go there.

I keep my thoughts from straying and check my watch. I have some time to go check out her vehicle. Maybe it will hold some clues.

Telling myself I'm not crossing any of the lines I've drawn for myself, I leave the empty apartment and make my way downstairs and out onto the sidewalk. I cross the street and head to her old Toyota.

I've never looked inside her car before, so I don't know what it normally looks like, but today the back seat is filled with cardboard boxes and plastic bags. Is she living out of her car? I would have known that, wouldn't I? The boxes hold toiletries, and the bags have her clothes. Does her car always look like this? Tell me she isn't a hoarder.

My shoulders draw tight because if I'd done more digging on Cin, I'd already know the answers to my questions. At the same time, if I go that far, I might never escape her.

I do another lap around the vehicle. When nothing else sticks out to me, I return to the apartment across the street. The last thing I need is to get caught skulking around the parking lot.

I keep watch on the bar, and about a half hour later, she reaches for her purse underneath the counter. She waves goodbye to the patrons sitting at the bar and leaves out the front door. I'm about to book it out of the apartment and to my car so I can follow her, but she diverges from her usual routine. She doesn't make her way immediately off the porch and over to the side lot to her car.

Instead, she flops down on one of the old chairs and leans over, putting her hands over her face.

Is she crying? My stomach twists, and the urge to run over and find out who made her upset and make them pay for it rises inside me. But if I do that, she'll wonder where I came from, and how do I explain that I've been across the road and watching her all day?

She raises her head, and I spot a tear track down her cheek.

My hands fist at my sides. I can't just stand here and do nothing.

I hurry out of the apartment, not bothering to lock the door, and rush down the stairs. Rather than take the front exit, I leave the building out the back and run behind all the buildings to the alleyway where I parked my car. Then I slowly creep onto Main Street and drive toward the bar.

Much to my relief, Cinder's still sitting in the chair. Her back is heaving, and she keeps wiping her cheeks. I'm not sure how I'm going to play this, but I pull up in front of the bar and slow my car to a stop, putting it in park before I climb out and walk along the front of the vehicle.

"Thought that was you," I say, trying to play off a nonchalance that is natural.

Her head whips up and her eyes widen. She wipes the tears from her cheeks with her fingers. "Nero, what are you doing here?"

Jesus, hearing my name on her lips is enough to undo me. It's only the pain in her eyes that keeps me in check and reminds me why I came here.

"What's wrong?" I take the three steps up onto the porch and crouch in front of her so I'm not lording over her.

"Just family stuff." She sniffles, and it's clear that she's trying to pull herself together.

But I want her a mess. I want to know all the ins and outs of this woman, especially what has her so upset. I want to fix her and the problem. But now isn't the time to push her. She needs to trust me first.

"I'm familiar with those."

Her head tilts. "Really?"

I nod and give her a small smile. "Unfortunately, yes. Anything I can help with?"

"You don't even know me. Why would you want to help me?" The way her big blue eyes stare into my own makes me think she really wants to know the answer to this question, and it's not a surface-level ask.

I'm not sure I can answer the question, so I say, "How could I not? I see a beautiful woman crying, and you expect me to just drive on by?"

She laughs.

"Seriously, though." I take one of her hands. "What can I do to help?"

Her hands are so small, and the heat from her soft skin seeps into mine despite the fact that it's cool out.

"I left my home because... I have nowhere to stay."

I frown. "Why did you leave?"

Her lip quivers. "My mom died when I was really young. My dad passed about a decade ago."

My eyes fall closed for a second. I know exactly what that feels like. When I open my eyes, there's raw pain in Cin's eyes. I love the juxtaposition of the confident, powerful woman on stage and the vulnerable one sitting in front of me. But I take no pleasure in her pain.

"Come home with me." The words leave my mouth before I consider them, but I don't regret saying them.

Her head rocks back. "You don't know me. I don't even really know you."

I let go of her hand and stand, shoving my hands in the pockets of my coat. "True, but I can tell you anything you need to know, and there's more than enough room at my house. You'd have your own room, your own space. You can stay as long as you'd like."

She shakes her head, standing and swinging her purse over her shoulder. "I appreciate the offer, but I don't even know if you're a serial killer or something."

I step closer to her and place my hand on her cheek. It feels impossible to be this close to her and not touch her. "Do you think I'm a serial killer?"

She holds my gaze and shakes her head. "No. No, I don't."

"Do you feel safe around me?" I hold my breath while I wait for her answer. I'm not sure why the question feels like a heavy weight.

Cin nods, although reluctantly it seems. "Oddly, yes."

"Then come home with me. At least for tonight. You have nowhere to go. We don't even have to interact if you don't want to. I'll leave you alone. But you can't expect me to just leave you here with nowhere to go."

She hems and haws, and I take her hand again and squeeze.

"Please. Just for tonight."

She nods. "Okay, for tonight."

I try to hold back my smile and not show her how happy her decision makes me. "Great, follow me to my place then."

"Alright."

I hurry down the steps and back into my car before she changes her mind.

Now I have to figure out how to get her to stay more than one night.

CHAPTER
TEN

CINDER

I follow Nero's expensive car, barely believing that I'm about to be welcomed into his home. My nerves make me edgy, and I keep having to clench and unclench my hands from around the steering wheel as we make our way up the hill to the manor at the top.

When he reaches a set of iron gates, he rolls down his window, presses a code into the keypad, and speaks into the speaker. He eases his car through the gates, and I follow him onto a tree-lined winding road.

The trees finally clear, and I'm met with a dark sprawling mansion so large I never imagined places like this existed. Mist hangs low to the ground, and an ominous feeling rises around me. For the first time since he asked me to come home with him, I have second thoughts.

There are two spires on each far end of the massive manor, and I spot points of two more off in the distance. The dark gray stone gives the place a Gothic feel, and I imagine this place standing here a thousand years ago, though that's impossible.

Nero parks his car in the circular drive, and I park beside him, sucking in a deep breath before I climb out.

He waits for me. "You can leave your things in your car. One of the staff will bring it to your room."

I nod, the word staff feeling overwhelming. You'd need a full team of people to run a place this big. And do they treat the staff the way Louise treats me? If so, I'm not sure I can handle that. But it's only for one night, and I have no other choice.

"When you said I could stay at your place, I didn't imagine it would look like *this*." I look up and spot stone gargoyles perched on top of the mansion. I swear their eyes are watching us, assessing, judging.

Nero chuckles. "It can be overwhelming. I didn't want you to say no."

My cheeks heat with his admission. "I'm only staying the night. I don't need all my things." I gesture to the back seat, where basically every belonging I own is packed.

"We'll discuss that later. Come on. Dinner is already underway. Let's get you something to eat."

I swallow back my nerves when he gestures toward the house and walks in that direction. A huge door with a stained-glass window draws my attention. Its beauty feels at odds with the heavy feeling of the rest of the building.

"This is Midnight Manor." Nero opens the door, and I step over the threshold, taking in the grandeur. "We're in the communal part of the manor, and four wings venture out. I'm in the south wing. We'll go there after we grab something to eat."

I turn to face him and nod, feeling overwhelmed by the display of wealth surrounding me. Each painting and piece of furniture is probably worth more than my dad's entire home.

"C'mon." He gestures for me to follow him.

The manor is dimly lit as we walk through the rooms and hallways. It's so large that I feel trapped in a maze, easily losing track of where we started.

I hear people's voices up ahead, and I realize that we're not just going into the kitchen to grab food and go to his section of the house. We're about to interrupt a meal in progress. He's got to be kidding me.

I tug on the sleeve of Nero's jacket, and he stops, giving me a quizzical look. "My name is Cinder. Cin is just what I go by when I... perform." I'm not sure why I feel self-conscious about telling him that, but I don't feel right about him introducing me to anyone by my stripper name.

He gives me a warm smile, seeming to understand. "Okay, Cinder."

We continue walking toward the voices until we come upon what's clearly a dining room.

"Finally, where the hell have you been?" Asher Voss asks. I recognize his voice from when he came into the bar a long time ago when Anabelle had some trouble there. He's as intimidating as the people say he is. The Voss family is well-known in Magnolia Bend, although not many people have had conversations with them.

"Sorry, I'm late. I, uh... had something that came up," Nero says.

I step around him to make my presence known.

"Guys, this is Cinder," Nero says, gesturing to me at his side.

"Oh my god! Cinder!" Anabelle bolts up from the table and rushes around to give me a hug. "I'm so happy to see you here."

Before Anabelle and Asher were married, she would come into the bar with her brother. We would chat while I worked, and she was always nice. When she found out I also worked at T&T's, she never gave me that judgmental look others did.

Rapsody gets up from the table, too, and gives me a hug. "It's so good to see you again."

I met her the one time she was in the bar with Anabelle, but she seems just as personable and nice.

"You too."

"We're just here to pick up food before we head to my wing," Nero says.

The cutest Labrador puppy crawls out from under the table and sniffs my feet.

"Oh my gosh, who is this?" I crouch down and pet the puppy.

"That's Max. Kol just gave him to me tonight," Rapsody says, squatting next to me.

"He is so sweet."

Max props up on his hind legs and licks my face. I laugh, petting him more.

"He sure likes you," Rapsody says, running her hand down his back.

I peek up, and Nero is watching me with a look I can't interpret. I gently ease Max off of me and stand, a tad embarrassed that I got carried away when I don't really know anyone here.

"You know Anabelle and Rapsody?" Nero asks.

"They've been in the bar."

"Right." Nero seems relieved by my answer, and the tension in his shoulders loosens.

"Hello, Cinder," Asher says, stepping forward, holding out his hand. "Good to see you again."

I nod, shaking his hand. Asher Voss is an intimidating presence. He came into the Black Magic Bar awhile back, insisting that if Anabelle was ever there and needed any assistance, I was to call him, which I only had to do one time.

"This is Obsidian, but everyone calls him Sid," Nero says and gestures to a man who isn't sitting with a woman next to him.

His suit looks as if it costs a small fortune, which makes the wolf tattoo on his neck surprising, not melding with his put-together exterior. His wavy brown hair is slicked back, and his dark eyes make me want to step back when he sticks his hand out for a handshake. But that would be rude and wouldn't endear me to Nero, so I accept his hand.

"Good to meet you, Cinder." His fathomless eyes meet mine, and I swear they're looking into my soul. I try to keep my eyes on his for as long as I can before I have to look away.

"And this is Kol," Rapsody says with a huge smile. "My fiancé."

Nero whips his head toward Kol. "You guys are engaged?"

"He asked me earlier tonight." She pushes her hand out to show the giant rock that sits on the ring finger of her left hand.

After Nero and I are done offering our congratulations, everyone else returns to their seats around the table, but Nero doesn't show me to a seat.

"We're going to make up some plates, then I'm showing Cinder to her room," Nero says.

"Will you be staying with us long?" Sid asks.

Nero's lips thin as he stares at his brother.

"Just tonight. Thank you for having me." I'd do just about anything to get out of this room. The feeling I had at my father's house washes over me—like a freeloading loafer. I can't imagine what his brothers must think. Nero bringing home the bartender and stripper from T&T's.

If Nero's look could kill, Sid would be splayed on the table, gutted and bleeding out.

"Get a plate from the sideboard and put on however much you want, Cinder."

I do as he says while Anabelle tries to stir up the conversation again around the table, which I appreciate. Once we each have a plate, Nero leads me out of the dining room without saying a word to his family.

I stop at the archway of the doorway. "Thank you."

All their eyes are on us with looks of confusion over fake smiles. It's only one night, and I'll probably never be back here again.

CHAPTER
ELEVEN

NERO

We walk through the communal part of the manor until we reach the long hallway that leads to my wing—the south wing. Each one of us boys have stained-glass windows displayed in our wings. Cinder stops with her plate in her hand.

She stops in front of mine—the raven. "This one is extraordinary."

"My mom had this one done before she died."

Cinder's eyes widen and find mine. "I'm sorry. I didn't realize your mom had passed."

"Both my parents are dead." It's just another thing that draws me to her, that she can understand how it feels to be orphaned as a child. She frowns, but I don't want to put a damper on tonight, so I motion ahead with my free hand. "C'mon. We're almost there."

I lead her down the hall and bring her to the bedroom she'll be staying in. It has the largest en suite bath, and besides my own master suite, it's the biggest room in my wing. I want Cinder to be comfortable so that she'll stay.

"This is your room." I walk over to the sofa and chairs and set my plate on the table.

Cinder places her plate next to mine and gazes around the room.

"Is the room okay?" I ask, taking in her wide-eyed expression.

"Of course. How could it not be? It's so huge and opulent. Compared to..."

Her voice trails off with a sad note. I fight with myself, wanting to make whatever it is better for her. I want to know what went down between her and her stepmother, but it's New Year's Eve, and it's her first night here. I want her to stay here for more than just tonight which means starting off on a good foot. We can discuss what happened tomorrow.

"You go sit and eat. I'm going to ask one of the staff to bring your belongings to the room."

She nods, clearly still deep in thought, and absentmindedly turns to sit on the couch, scooting to the edge so she can eat over her plate.

I pull my phone from my pants and text Marcel to have someone bring her things from her car before I take a seat beside her.

We eat in silence for a few minutes, the only sound is the scraping of forks and knives on the plates.

"Sorry it's cold. If we'd been here earlier, it would have tasted better."

She shrugs. "I don't mind. I'm used to it."

Again, questions plague my mind to what she's been through, but I tell myself to save my questions so I don't overwhelm her and send her running.

"Can I ask you something?" she says, breaking the silence.

I finish chewing and swallow. "Of course."

"In the dining room, you seemed a little thrown that your brother and Rapsody were engaged. Do you think they shouldn't be?"

Do I tell Cinder about how I broke off my engagement, or do I keep it to myself? Will it scare her away if she knows I was an engaged man only six months ago? I decide that much like whatever went down with her and her stepmom, that topic is for a later discussion.

"I just wasn't expecting it, that's all. Kol hadn't mentioned anything."

"I see. Do you like Rapsody and Anabelle? They seem really nice from the little I know them."

I cut into my meat and nod. "Yeah, they're both great. We didn't have the easiest childhood, and in some ways that left each of us a little damaged, but... I don't know. I think they give my brothers comfort and make them happy."

I'm surprised I admitted what I did about my childhood. I never broached that topic with Maude.

There's a look of concern on Cinder's face, but there's also understanding. Did she have a hard childhood too?

"Anyway, seems like there will be another wedding in the Voss family. Asher and Anabelle were married last spring."

She smiles and goes back to eating her meal.

There's a knock at the door. When I say come in, Marcel pokes his head in. "Where would you like our guest's belongings?"

I motion toward the door of the walk-in closet. "You can put them in the closet please. Marcel, this is Cinder. Cinder, this is Marcel, the house manager."

"Pleasure to meet you." He nods in deference as he comes in with plastic bags in hand.

"You too," Cinder says. Her cheeks grow pink as she looks at the bags before turning away.

Marcel returns from the closet moments later. "I'll return with the rest."

After the door shuts, I place my silverware on my plate. "What's wrong?"

"Well... what must he think about everything I own being in plastic bags and cardboard boxes? I'm sure he's used to bringing in designer leather luggage."

"Hey." I place my finger and thumb on her chin, bringing her face to mine. "First of all, until Anabelle and Rapsody,

92

we didn't have guests sleep here. Ever. And second, Marcel doesn't judge, and neither do I."

Tears fill her eyes. "Why are you being so nice to me?"

My gaze roams over her beautiful face. What do I tell her? That I've been obsessed with her from the minute I saw her? That I've been secretly stalking her for months? That I feel this intense pull to her that I can't explain?

I can't tell her any of that.

"Don't worry about that. We'll figure things out in the morning."

She nods, and the kind, genuinely thankful expression on her face makes me want to wrap her in my arms and promise her the world.

Instead, I pop up off the couch. "I'm going to bring these plates back to the kitchen. I'll be back to check on you."

"Oh, I'm happy to take them."

My forehead wrinkles. "Nonsense. You're my guest. Just relax, and get settled. I'll be back in a bit."

"Okay," she says softly.

I pick up the dirty dishes and leave the room, taking a deep breath when I reach the hallway, and I'm no longer surrounded by her jasmine and sandalwood scent.

The dining room is empty, and when I enter the kitchen, the staff are finishing the cleanup. I pass the dishes to them and thank everyone for dinner.

As soon as I enter the hallway, Sid's waiting for me at the far end with his arms crossed.

"Is the missus all settled?" He arches an eyebrow.

"Funny." I continue to walk past him, but he steps in front of me.

"First you stalk her, then you bring her home. Seems like things are escalating."

"She got kicked out of her place and had nowhere to go. What was I supposed to do?"

His arms fall to his sides. "Let her figure it out like the adult she is."

I shrug. "Maybe that works for you."

"You're walking on a tightrope, kid."

I grit my teeth. "I have it under control."

He steps closer, and his breath reeks of alcohol. "Do you think she'd have come here so willingly if she knew that her host is her stalker?"

I shove him with both hands, and he stumbles back a few steps. "Don't even think of telling her. And it's not stalking since I never followed her home, and I didn't trace her online activity."

He chuckles. "Keep telling yourself that." He walks past me in the direction from which I came.

A big part of me wants to chase him down the hall and beat him, telling him not to worry about me. That he and our other two brothers don't need to look out for me, but the quicksand of my guilt keeps me in place. They protected me when we were young, especially Sid, who took the brunt of our dad's beatings to save me. That guilt doesn't allow me to tell them to stop protecting me now.

I can't show up to Cinder's room with my head a mess from the past, so I retreat to my own room, shaking off the feeling. It's an hour later before I return to Cinder's room. The door is open, and Cinder is pacing the room.

"Sorry I took so long. I had to deal with something."

"That's okay. I'm sorry for interrupting your evening."

I step farther into the room until I'm standing in front of her. "You're not interrupting anything."

"But it's New Year's Eve. You probably have plans. Please don't let me prevent you from—"

I place my finger over her lips. "I'm exactly where I want to be."

Our gazes lock and hold. I remove my finger when I really want to slide my thumb into her mouth, then run the wetness over her lips.

"Are you sure?"

"I'm sure. Speaking of New Year's Eve." I flip my wrist to check the time. "There's only two minutes until midnight. We can ring in the New Year together."

"Oh… okay," she whispers.

Our eyes don't stray from the other's until I check my watch again.

"Five… four… three… two… one." I bring my hand to her face and entwine it in her hair. "Happy New Year." I bring my lips to hers even though I shouldn't push her too fast.

But when our lips meet, it's an instant inferno rather than a slow-building fire. I wrap my other arm around her waist, pulling her into my chest. She opens her mouth for me, and I finally get my first taste of her after months of wondering if it would be as good as I imagined. Fuck, it's even better.

Our tongues tangle, and she cedes control to me, letting me lead. I deepen the kiss, and though I want my hands all over her body, I don't want to push my luck. I need her to want to stay here for more than just tonight.

Eventually, I force myself to unwrap my arms from around her and close the kiss.

"Happy New Year," I say.

"Happy New Year."

What a perfect way to start the new year and put the shitty year behind me. Maybe it's an omen that this year will be better than the last.

CHAPTER
TWELVE

CINDER

When I wake up, it takes me a moment to remember where I am. I sit up in a big, cushy bed and take in all the opulence surrounding me. It makes the ache for home lessen.

It's hard to think about my family estate, knowing I'll never step foot in there again. But the good feelings about it have been fading over the years, replaced with shitty memories. I despise Louise and my stepsisters for stealing away my happy memories until they are mere whispers in the walls of my family home.

I still can't believe Nero invited me to stay here. I knew the Voss family was rich of course, mega rich, and I've heard the stories, urban legends, but I never would have conjured up this manor in my mind.

I'm so used to being up early to get things done around the house that the sun is rising as I slide out of bed. Unsure what to do with myself, I shower and dress for the day. Since it would be weird for me to wander around the manor, I decide to hang out until Nero seeks me out.

I check my cell phone for any text messages, but there's nothing. It's early, but Louise must not have seen my message from last night telling her that I won't ever be returning to the estate again. I wish I could see the look on her face when she realizes there's going to be no one to do their bidding and hand them money every day.

It's hard to stay still. I'm not accustomed to not having a list of tasks to accomplish, so I'm thankful when there's a soft knock at the door.

I rush over and swing the door open. Nero is standing on the other side, dressed casually in a pair of black jeans and white T-shirt with a brown suede jacket over the top. His blue eyes dip down then back up, taking me in, and a shiver runs up my spine.

"Good morning," I say with a smile and step back, inviting him inside.

"How'd you sleep last night?"

"Like the dead."

I smile, but Nero's eyes widen, and it takes him a moment to recover.

"Good. Are you hungry for breakfast? I thought we could eat together."

I am hungry, and more than that, that idea of being able to sit and enjoy my breakfast, rather than shoving something in my mouth as I'm doing chores around the house, is even more appealing. My first hot home-cooked meal in... I have no idea how long.

"I'd like that."

Nero leads me out into the wide hallway with high arching ceilings. Even though it's morning, the space still has an oppressive feel. It doesn't take long before he gestures for me to go through a door on his left.

Inside is a small—by Midnight Manor standards—kitchen with the basics. The far corner has a little breakfast nook with benches that have been upholstered in a rich red and black fabric and are surrounded by three intricate arched windows.

"I had this room renovated into a kitchen so I don't have to hike to the main kitchen every time I want a snack or something to drink."

I smile and sit at the table, where plates of pastries, fruit, and yogurt are on display. "Oh, I don't know. You could definitely get your ten thousand steps in a day walking back and forth to the main kitchen every time you're thirsty."

He chuckles and sits beside me. "True enough. Is this okay for breakfast? I can have something else brought if you prefer."

I wave off his concern. "This is perfect, thanks."

"Coffee?" he asks, picking up a carafe.

"No, thanks. I don't drink coffee."

He looks momentarily stunned. "How can anyone not drink coffee first thing in the morning?"

I just smile and don't bother telling him it's because Louise always insisted on having a very expensive coffee imported, and therefore I was never permitted to have any, so I never got addicted like my stepsisters.

We eat in silence, but it doesn't feel uncomfortable like I thought it might. No, like most things with this man, I'm entirely comfortable. *Too* comfortable even.

Eventually, he breaks the silence. "Now that you've had a good night's sleep, I wondered... why do you feel as though you can't go home?"

I expected this question. I suppose now is as good a time as any. I finish chewing my croissant and meet his gaze. "My dad died when I was fifteen, and that's when everything changed. I'd always known that my stepmother didn't care for me, even when my dad was alive. But somehow, he was happy with her, so I never said a word. I wanted him to be happy. There are images in my mind from after my mom died of my father's devastation, so I was glad he found someone to make him smile again. But she never cared for me, nor did my stepsisters. Once Dad was gone, they were free to make it known how much they actually despised me."

I blink back tears desperate to fall from talking about my dad. Nero squeezes my hand.

I sniffle and suck in a big breath. "Anyway, they've made my life a living hell for years, and I stuck around because I didn't want to leave the only home I'd ever known. That place used to hold such good memories for me, you know? But my stepmom grew more and more demanding of my time, my money, my energy until I just broke. I lashed out at her a few days ago, and New Year's Eve, that was it. Before I left for work I packed up what I could, knowing I couldn't stay there any longer and texted her to tell her I'd never be coming back." I shrug as though that's all there is to say about the topic.

"You said he passed when you were fifteen. How old are you now?"

I give him a watery smile. "I'll be twenty-five in a couple weeks."

I'd never tell him, but I looked him up online after my lap dance. I already know he's thirty-one.

"What day is your birthday?"

When I tell him, he nods.

"What's your plan then?" he asks.

I guess I've overstayed my welcome. Panic grips me on where I'll go, but I play it off with a shrug. He said one night. I agreed to one night. Now it's time for me to leave.

"Not sure. I'll figure something out."

He takes my hand. "Stay here."

I shake my head. "I've already taken advantage of your hospitality. You don't even know me, yet you let me spend the night in your home."

"But I want to know you. That's what I'm saying. And I *need* to know that you're okay and have somewhere safe to live."

"Nero, I appreciate the offer—"

"Please, Cinder. You have nowhere else to go, and as you can see, there's plenty of space here." When I don't say anything, he adds, "Just until you're back on your feet."

"Nero, I don't know…"

"Cinder, I'm not going to take no for an answer." His voice is different. Usually, it's deep and calm, reassuring. But now it's as if he leaves no room for argument. He's domineering and demanding, and I don't hate it.

I nod. "Okay. Just until I figure something out."

His entire countenance changes, and he relaxes back into his seat. "Good. I'm glad we have that squared away. Are you finished eating? I want to show you something."

I pluck a grape off my plate and toss it in my mouth. "Yes, I'm stuffed."

He slides out of the bench, and I follow suit. Without preamble, he takes my hand to lead me through the manor. I'm surprised by how natural it feels, how normal, and how good.

He leads me around, and once again I lose my sense of direction in this monstrous place. I spare glances at the expensive art that looks as if it's been here for centuries, the soaring ceilings, and the arched and intricate windows that the light has trouble penetrating.

We pass a set of double doors that sit wide open, and I gasp when I see what's inside and stop in the doorway.

Nero's hand drops and gestures toward the doors. "Did you want to see the ballroom? It never gets used. Back when my parents were alive, my brothers tell me they'd have parties in there, but I don't remember."

"Do you mind?" I take a hesitant step forward.

"Of course not. Come on." He walks into the room, and I follow.

My gaze bounces around, finding it difficult to take in all the grandeur. Stone columns flank each side, and once I pass them, I'm on the dance floor. The other side of the columns must be where people chat and sip their drinks during a party. Above me, the ceiling must be forty or fifty feet high and has painted motifs in each section. It reminds me of something you'd see in Europe from centuries past. Enormous glass chandeliers line the space, though they're not lit. Light filters in through the huge windows on the far side of the columns.

I circle around, twirling with my arms out. "This is magnificent. I can't imagine what it would be like to dance in here."

I stop spinning, almost giddy, and look at Nero. His head is tilted, and he's studying me.

"I'm going to guess that you enjoy dancing?"

My cheeks heat from not playing it cool. "I used to dance before my dad passed. After that, my stepmother wouldn't let me. I loved it though."

"You miss it." He steps toward me.

I try to fight my frown, but I do. "That's just one of many things I miss."

"You're welcome to use this space any time you like. Despite it never being used, the sound system has been kept up to date. You can just plug your phone in and play whatever you want. It's all over in that corner." He gestures behind me with his arm.

"Maybe." The urge to rush over and put something on for me to dance to, just for me and no one else, is fierce inside me. It's a stark reminder of everything Louise has taken from me over the years. With one last look around the space, I turn to Nero. "Now, what did you want to show me?"

He takes my hand, warmth spreading up my arm, and we leave the ballroom. "I don't think it's going to impress you quite as much as the ballroom just did."

I chuckle. "I'm sure you're wrong. This entire place is impressive."

We walk for another minute or so before Nero leads me into a room, closing the door behind us.

"This is my aviary," he says with pride in his voice.

The room is almost all glass walls with arched windows that match the architecture of the house. There are plants everywhere and perches set up for the host of birds. Their chirping fills the space.

"Wow, how many birds are in here?" I gaze at the glass ceiling and spot birds flying around.

Suddenly, a bird flies out of a nearby tree and lands on my shoulder.

I freeze, eyes wide and beseeching. "What do I do?"

Nero chuckles. "Nothing, just relax."

Slowly I relax my shoulders, and they drop.

"He likes you," Nero says. "He usually comes to me."

I turn my head and see that the bird is mostly blue with a reddish-brown breast. "He's really pretty."

"That's the Eastern Bluebird." He smiles.

"Are they all this friendly?"

He chuckles and steps forward with his arm out. "Come on, buddy, I think you're freaking poor Cinder out."

As though the bird understands him, he hops down off my shoulder and onto Nero's extended arm.

"What's your favorite bird?"

He doesn't even take a moment to think of his answer. "The raven."

I think back to the stained-glass raven we pass coming in and out of the south wing. "What made you want to collect birds?"

He walks farther into the space. "I don't think of it as collecting. I've always liked birds. Since I was young, after I took in a bird that had been injured in the wild. I cared for it and then others, one rescue after another. Ones who probably can't go back out into the wild and survive and need someone to look out for them, protect them."

I'm realizing there's more to Nero than meets the eye. There's a waver in his voice, almost as though he understands what it's like to need protection.

"You're a good man, Nero." The truthful words escape my lips.

He lifts his hand, and the bird flies off. "You wouldn't think that if you really knew me."

I meet his crystal gaze. "I already do."

CHAPTER
THIRTEEN

NERO

It's been almost a week since Cinder moved into Midnight Manor. I've tried to give her space and instructed the staff to bring her meals rather than force her to sit with my family in the dining room. At this point, I don't trust my brothers not to cause issues.

I've seen her briefly, checking in to make sure everything is okay and that she has everything she needs. Of course, I still follow her any time she leaves the house. I watch her from afar, including the booth at T&T's. We don't discuss the fact I'm there, nor do we discuss what happened in the VIP room. It's an unspoken agreement between us that we both seem to understand.

But every day, I grow more and more desperate to get closer to her. To touch her, feel her, and taste her.

So on my way to the aviary one afternoon, when I pass by the ballroom and hear music, I come to a stop. I sneak in through the doors and hide behind a column. I recognize the song playing as "Praying" by Kesha.

Cinder's hair is pulled back into a low ponytail. The leggings and sports bra she's wearing make my dick press against the zipper of my slacks. God, her fucking tits. She ebbs and flows to the music, her body and movements almost becoming one with the beat. My eyes fixate, unable to look away.

I knew she was flexible from seeing her at the strip club, but there she's more rehearsed. She rolls and bends and stretches to the beat as if she feels the rhythm. At the club, she's confident and powerful, a woman owning her destiny despite the dingy surroundings. But here amid all the wealth and grandeur, she appears vulnerable.

Her beauty tugs deep inside me, some younger version of myself that I sealed away decades ago. Watching her, that little boy, the one who was terrified of his father, who can barely remember the love of his mother, rises. Pressure builds behind my eyes, and they water—for what was, what could have been, and what never will be.

I could watch her dance all day. All night. Fucking forever.

That word is all I think about when it comes to Cinder. Forever.

I shake my head.

What the hell am I thinking? I need this obsession with her to fizzle out, but everything about her is like taking fans to flames, turning it into an inferno. Did I not learn my lesson with Maude?

The song crescendos, and she's like a woman possessed. All the emotion in the lyrics is displayed in every movement of her body, and if it weren't clear to me before, it is now. This woman is just as familiar with deep trauma and pain as I am.

The question is, do I want to dig up and examine her pain, try to help her get over the past? I remind myself that's the kind of thing a man in love would do, and this is not that. No, this is a fleeting obsession that will eventually burn out.

The song slows to a close, and tears track down her face as she collapses onto the floor, staring at the ceiling. Another song that I don't recognize plays, and Cinder doesn't get up to dance. Instead, she curves in on herself and weeps.

It almost kills me to walk away from her in that condition. But I know myself. I can feel my obsession building and gaining more strength.

What Maude did to me messed me up, and I didn't feel for her a fraction of what I do for Cinder. I don't know how that's possible, but it is. I just need some space from Cinder to get my head in order. Then I can be around her again and not risk completely falling for her.

Wanting to fuck her is one thing. Wanting to love her is quite another.

So I leave her crying in the ballroom, as much as it pains me, knowing it's for the best.

WHEN I ENTER the dining room that evening for dinner, I'm a little late, so I'm surprised to find Anabelle sitting alone.

"Where's everyone else?" I ask, sliding into my seat.

"Asher got stuck on a call. Should join us soon. No idea where everyone else is."

"Think Ash will be pissed if just the two of us dine together? Like a date?" I waggle my eyebrows.

Anabelle chuckles and shakes her head. "As much as you'd probably love to annoy your brother like that, I think he'll be fine."

I dish a few items onto my plate. "How's married life by the way?" It feels a little awkward bringing up marriage, given that I too was supposed to be able to answer that question by now.

Anabelle pauses while cutting up her meat. "Pretty much the same as pre-married life, honestly." She shrugs.

"So Asher's still a miserable prick, and you're still Suzie Sunshine." I stab my salad with a fork.

Anabelle tilts her head as though I'm a misbehaving student, and she's the teacher ready to discipline. "He's not a prick. I like to think he's... misunderstood most of the time."

I laugh. "Sure, that's it."

Anabelle shakes her head. "How's Cinder settling in?"

I try to refrain from showing emotion at the mention of Cinder's name. "Haven't seen that much of her, but fine."

Anabelle frowns. "You haven't spent any time with her?"

I shrug and reach for the wine bottle to fill my glass. "Why would I?"

She sets down her cutlery and leans back in her chair, her hands clasped together. "You wouldn't have brought her to live here if you didn't have some interest in her."

I bring the wine glass to my lips, taking a large gulp to buy myself some time. Anabelle watches me intently, her eyebrows raised to let me know she's waiting for me to answer.

I put down the wine glass and wipe my mouth with my napkin. "Maybe I was just being a good guy and trying to help out someone in need."

My answer doesn't appease her because she gives me a "yeah right" expression. "If that were the case, you could've given her some money and sent her on her way."

Damn her, she has a good point.

"I'm trying to make sure things remain uncomplicated."

Anabelle laughs. "Everything about love is complicated."

I scoff. "Who said anything about love?"

She gives me another expression to say she doesn't buy what I'm selling. "Maybe not yet, but maybe there's the possibility it could grow between you two. I liked Cinder from the moment I met her at Black Magic Bar."

What's not to like? I've been obsessed with her since the moment I saw her at T&T's, I think but don't say.

"Just because you found your happily ever after doesn't mean we're all destined for the same." I shove a mouthful of salad in my mouth, done with this conversation.

Anabelle must be able to tell, because we eat in silence for a few minutes.

"You know Cinder's birthday is coming up in a couple days. She mentioned it when we were chatting at Black Magic."

I don't say anything but continue to eat my meal. I know her fucking birthday is coming up.

"It would be such a shame if she had to celebrate it on her own. In this big, strange house that she doesn't know." She lifts her wineglass to her lips. "Just saying."

I know what she's trying to do. I know, and yet damn it, it's working. I hate the idea of Cinder feeling as if no one cares enough to acknowledge her birthday. Has anyone *ever* done something special on her birthday? Something tells me the answer is not in a very long time.

I sit, continuing to eat and trying to let it go. To not care what Cinder does for her birthday. But it's like an itch under my skin that I can't quite reach. And by the time Asher walks in to join us, I know what I'm going to do despite my need for self-preservation.

"Sorry that took so long." He stops at the end of the table and looks around the room. "Just the three of us tonight?"

I set my napkin on the table and push my chair out to stand. "Just the two of you. I have something I need to go do." Anabelle gives me a cheeky grin, and I roll my eyes. "See you two later."

"The more over the top, the better," Anabelle calls out, laughing.

I flip her off right before leaving the room.

"What was that about?" Asher asks her.

Oh, nothing. Your youngest brother is just choosing torture over self-preservation, Ash. Nothing to see here. Nothing at all.

CHAPTER
FOURTEEN

CINDER

For the first time in my adult life, I've taken my birthday off. I won't be slinging drinks or shaking my tits today. I'll be able to do whatever I want, though as I lie in bed staring at the ceiling, I have no idea what that might be.

Nero has avoided me for the past week, for reasons I'm not sure of. The first week I was here, he was checking on me, but he's been especially MIA this past week.

I took him up on his offer of using the ballroom to dance. Which is definitely something I could do today. Dancing for myself has been so cathartic.

There's a knock at my door, and I sit up, holding the sheet to my chest. "Come in."

I expect it to be Marcel with my breakfast tray, but Nero walks through the door with the tray.

He smiles. "Good morning, and happy birthday."

He remembered. That alone fills my eyes with wetness. No one in my life has acknowledged my birthday since my dad.

"Thank you."

He sets the tray on the table before sitting on the edge of the bed. His scent wraps around me, and I want to lean in to smell him better, but I don't. He's clearly been wary of me lately, and I don't want to push it.

"Do you have any plans for the day?"

I'm embarrassed to admit that I don't. "Not really, no."

"I was hoping you'd say that. Eat up, and in about an hour, I have people coming here to see you. I made plans for us tonight."

My chest fills with a warm feeling I can only remember from when I was young and in the presence of my parents. "What plans? Who's coming here?"

"Don't worry. Just answer the knock on the door in an hour. I'll see you tonight." He leans in as though maybe he's going to kiss me, but then seems to think better of it and stands from the bed.

I watch him leave the room, wondering what this turnabout could possibly be about and not really caring because it's what I hoped for.

A LITTLE MORE THAN an hour later, there's a knock at the bedroom door. Though I had no idea who to expect, I was not expecting three people to be standing there when I open the door.

"Cinder?" the woman at the front with bright red hair that's clearly dyed and one side of her head shaved asks.

"Yes..."

"Perfect. Mind giving us some room so we can get all this stuff in here?"

That's when I notice some of the house staff, including Marcel, behind the three strangers. They carry boxes or bags and two of them even have a rolling rack of clothes.

"I'm confused. What's going on?" I stand stunned while Marcel circles around the three of them.

"Mr. Voss insisted that these"—he side-eyes the three people—"kind people get you ready for this evening. Along with filling your closet with a whole new wardrobe that is befitting of your beauty." When I don't say anything, he gives me a kind smile. "Why don't you let them step inside and get set up while you take your time to wrap your head around things?"

I nod absentmindedly and swing the door open farther, stepping out of their way.

It takes fifteen minutes for them to get everything into the room and organized. I sit on one of the chairs and watch.

Marcel walks over to me. "I'm going to leave them to it, but if you have any issues at all, let me know."

"Okay. Thank you, Marcel. I can't believe Nero is doing all of this for me." Tears prick my eyes. No one has done anything nice like this for me since... well, since Nero let me stay here, I suppose.

He gives me a smile. "I can." Then he bids farewell to the strangers.

I rise off the chair and walk over to them. "As you can tell, I had no idea this was happening."

The red-haired woman laughs. "Yeah, that was pretty obvious. I'm Jaycee, and I'm here to do your makeup. This is Trent." She points at the gentleman with a barrel chest and close-cropped hair beside her. "He's going to do your hair, and Serena is in charge of style."

The woman with sleek black hair parted down the middle and dressed stylishly raises her hand in hello.

I return the gesture. "Hello, everyone. It's good to meet you."

"Why don't we get started with clothes first?" Serena says. Even though she's smiling, I can tell that this woman is all business.

"Okay, but I don't know what the plan is for tonight, so I'm not sure I'll be much help."

"We all have instructions," Jaycee says.

"Besides, I'm not just outfitting you for tonight. I've been instructed to fill your closet with clothes you like, so we have a lot to get through."

Nero asked for her to do that? I can't imagine how much that's going to cost because I can tell from the fabric hanging on the racks that these are all designer pieces.

My stomach whooshes. "Wow."

"Wow is right," Jaycee says. "I'm going to set up my retractable table and get everything together while you and Serena work on the fashion end."

"Same," Trent says.

They both head off to the other side of the room, leaving me with Serena.

"Let's go through some things to see what kind of style you like. You're very well-endowed, so it might mean sizing up for some items and having them tailored, but I work with the best in the business. I can have anything we need in a different size here within a couple of days."

"Um... okay, great."

We spend the next several hours together while Jaycee and Trent mill around patiently. I guess when getting paid whatever Nero is paying them, you don't complain about being bored.

At first, it was overwhelming, but it's become fun. It's like playing dress-up, only everything I like, I get to keep. No longer will I be wearing clothes I've had to mend to preserve or dated outfits because I didn't want to spend what little money I had to update them. I'll be dressed in the best clothes money can buy. All because of Nero.

Tears prick my eyes when I think of him. No one has ever treated me like this. It's hard to wrap my head around why he's being so nice to me. Does he want something from me too?

I still don't know what we're doing tonight, but Serena told me that I was to be dressed up, and we picked a blue silk floor-length dress. The fabric drapes to one side of my waist, then falls with a big slit down my right leg. I felt sexy the minute the silky fabric slid up my body. The slit isn't noticeable when I'm standing still, but as soon as I walk, my leg peek-a-boos.

By the time Serena is done, the closet is half full of beautiful clothes, the rest arriving over the coming days after they're tailored to my measurements. The items include all kinds of La Perla bras and underwear. She made it a point to say that Nero wanted to make sure that she didn't forget my intimates, and I kind of hope it's because he wants to see me in them.

I like that idea. He hasn't brought up what happened at the club or the New Year's Eve kiss we shared a couple of weeks ago. I'd assumed that's because he regretted them, but maybe that's not the case if he's having his stylist fit me for beautiful intimates.

Trent calls me over next to get my hair done, and since I don't color my hair, and I like my natural blonde, we settle on freshening up the ends. He also does a treatment on my hair that leaves it as smooth and shiny as my dress. Then he parts my hair off to one side, leaving it down and styled in Hollywood waves.

Next up is Jaycee, who brings my look all together, doing my makeup in a way that makes me feel prettier than I ever have. It's noticeable, but not overdone at the same time.

I look in the mirror at myself in wonder. "You three are miracle workers."

They all laugh, and Jaycee squeezes my shoulder from where she stands behind me in the mirror. "We had a great canvas to work with. Mr. Voss is going to be bowled over when he sees you."

My cheeks heat, and I look away from her gaze in the mirror.

"Don't worry, we all had to sign NDAs and hand in our phones. Unless we want our grandkids to still be paying off a judgment, we're all going to keep our mouths shut. Your secret is safe with us," Jaycee says.

I don't know whether she's referring to the fact that I obviously live here, or if she thinks Nero is my lover or maybe my sugar daddy. Maybe she knows I'm a stripper somehow and realizes how bad it would look for Nero to be tied to me publicly. Who knows?

I smile at her in the mirror.

"Is there anything you need before we get going? Do you want me to help you get into your dress?" Serena asks.

"I'm okay to do it on my own. Thank you so much for your help, everyone. I had such a fun day. I've never done anything like this before, which I'm sure you could tell."

"We hope you have a lovely evening," Serena says.

I do too. But it doesn't matter what happens for the rest of this night because one thing is for sure—this is already the best birthday I've ever had.

CHAPTER
FIFTEEN

NERO

I smooth down the front of my black silk three-piece suit, walking toward Cinder's room.

I'm nervous for the first time since I proposed to Maude over a year ago. Almost to the point of being jittery.

A lot is riding on tonight. At least it feels that way. I want Cinder to enjoy herself and remember this birthday for years to come. I want her to want to stay at the manor. She hasn't mentioned leaving again, but I'm sure it's only a matter of time. And I want her to see what it could be like between us if we both allowed ourselves to fall into this attraction we feel for each other.

I knock on her bedroom door and wait for her to answer. As soon as the door opens, and she's standing in front of me, all the air leaves my lungs in a rush. I stagger back, so struck by her beauty, I can't stop staring.

"Cinder, you look like a queen."

Her hair is down in waves, and the blue silk dress reveals a decent amount of cleavage, but it's her right leg sticking out of the slit in the dress that draws my attention. I want to run my hands up her leg, trail kisses up her inner thigh until I reach the apex of her thighs, then I want to make her scream with my mouth. I want to unravel this beautiful package in front of me until she's a begging, wanton mess —for me.

I shift my stance to hide the evidence of how my body reacts when I see her.

"Thank you." Her cheeks pinken, and it's fucking adorable. Amazing that giving her a compliment makes her blush, but dancing naked in front of a bunch of horny men doesn't do much.

"Are you ready for your surprise?" I hold my arm out to her, and she loops her arm through it.

"Do I need to bring anything with me?" she asks before we leave the room.

"Just yourself."

She smiles, and I lead her through the manor. If she has any idea of where we're headed, she gives no indication, but when we head down the hall with the ballroom, her hand twitches on my arm.

Music is already playing at a low level inside. I put together a playlist that I thought she might like and one we can slow dance to after dinner.

"We're going in here?" she asks.

I push open the door and lead her inside. She stops on the spot when she sees what awaits us.

I've had the entire room decorated for a birthday party. Spared no expense between the flowers and the balloons, the ice sculpture, and everything else the event planner suggested. The room appears as if we're expecting five hundred guests, but it will just be the two of us tonight.

She walks in front of me, twirling around, her eyes scouring every nook and cranny. "Nero... I have no words."

"Happy birthday." I lead her by the hand to the table in the center of the cavernous room, which is set for dinner for two. I hold out the chair for her, and I hold back the urge to kiss the nape of her neck.

I slide into the seat across from her and pick up the bottle of wine. "Would you like some wine?"

"Yes, please." She can't keep her gaze on one place, taking in the room, and I smile as I pour her a glass and pass it to her. She takes a sip. "Mmm, that's good."

"You say that like you've never tasted wine before."

Her gaze dips to the table. "I haven't. I... my stepmother wouldn't let me. I didn't even get to eat dinner with her and my stepsisters. I had to eat alone in my room. And I make it a rule not to drink at the club or the bar."

Anger fires up in my veins that someone could treat her like that. But I don't want to get into the shitty things she's had to endure. Tonight is for Cinder to be happy and carefree, not worrying about anything other than enjoying herself.

"Well then, I'm glad you like it, and I'm glad your first experience was with me. Shall we toast?"

"Okay." She raises her glass.

"To beginnings and whatever the future holds."

She clinks her glass to mine, a smile playing on her lips. "To beginnings."

We each take a sip, then one of the staff enters with our appetizers, setting a plate in front of each of us. As we work our way through the courses, we chat about nothing of much significance. Cinder asks about my job and what I do for Voss Enterprises, and I find out that she used to compete in dancing and that contemporary dance was her favorite.

She sets her spoon on her plate beside the half-eaten chocolate mousse. "I can't possibly eat another mouthful."

I chuckle. "Stuffed?"

"Completely." She places her hands over her belly. "Nero, thank you for today. Everything was so amazing. Thank you doesn't even feel adequate. This is the best birthday I can remember in a long time."

A buoyancy bounces inside me at her words. "What did you do for your birthday when you were a child?"

"Before my mom died, she would take me to a spa and let me get my nails painted. Even when I was little. I remember the feeling of being pretty. She'd let me pick out a new dress, whichever one I wanted, then we'd meet my dad for dinner at a restaurant. I was a princess for a day." The expression on her face tells me what the memories mean to her.

"And after she passed?"

Cinder sighs. "My dad tried for the first few years. He'd let me have some friends from school over for a birthday party. I missed the day of pampering with my mom, and it was never the same, but it was better than spending the day alone. Those parties stopped after my stepmother moved in. She claimed all the noise from the kids made her too stressed and anxious. Then after my dad passed, she stopped acknowledging my birthday altogether."

My hand tightens around my spoon. "You're never going back to that place."

She gives me a sad smile. "It's the only home I've ever known, but I've realized over the past few months that it may not be the place for me anymore."

Our gazes meet, and I want so badly to tell her that this can be her home, but I stop myself, not wanting to scare her off.

"Your mom sounds like a special person," I say.

She nods. "She really was."

"My mom died when I was six." Why am I telling her this? "I only remember little snippets of her, vague impressions. Sometimes I don't know if that's worse than remembering every little thing and grieving the loss."

Cinder takes my hand. "That must be really hard. It's painful, but I wouldn't give up my memories of my mom for anything."

I squeeze her small hand. "We don't talk about her a lot, but when my brothers do speak of her, I often feel like the odd man out. They have such vivid memories and speak so highly of her, but me... my memories are more feelings than anything else. How I felt when she was around me. That's what I miss most." God knows I never got the feeling of unconditional love from my father.

Cinder pulls her hand from mine, and I have an obsessive need to reconnect us, but I hold back.

"How did she pass? If you don't mind me asking."

I force my voice to sound lighter to not ruin this night. "She was murdered here at the manor, in the garden."

Her hand goes to her chest and sympathy floods in her eyes. "That's awful. I'm so sorry."

I nod. "It is." Getting sick of the heavy weight in my heart, I push my chair back and stand. "Care to dance?"

Her eyes sparkle, and she nods. Let's push that shit away for tonight.

She tracks me as I round the small table, going to the back of her chair and pulling it out. Then I extend a hand. She stands, and I lead her to the dance floor as a new song begins.

I take her hand and wrap my other arm around her small waist, tugging her into me, and we circle around the dance floor. I can't look away from her as we move perfectly in sync.

Something feels vaguely familiar, but I can't place why.

She moves effortlessly, and for the first time in a long time, I feel centered and whole with her in my arms. I'm starting to think this is more than just an obsession.

The song ends, and my present for her in my jacket pocket grows heavy. I brought it with me, but I wasn't sure I should give it to her. I don't want to come on too strong and scare her away. But I really want her to have it.

Another song starts and I pull back enough to look into her eyes. "I have a present for you."

She blinks a couple of times. "I think this whole day was present enough."

I shake my head. "Almost." I let go of her and step back. "Turn around."

Her forehead creases. "What for?"

I chuckle. "Do you want your present?"

She does as I ask, and I step closer to her, breathing in her jasmine and sandalwood scent. Reaching into the inside pocket of my jacket, I pull out a diamond necklace with a huge center sapphire that dangles down. With my free hand, I position her hair over one shoulder.

It would be so easy to lean forward and kiss the spot where her neck meets her shoulder, to taste her skin. Somehow, I find the willpower to resist once again.

"Close your eyes," I whisper in her ear, and her skin prickles with goosebumps.

I wind the necklace around her neck and attach it with the clasp, then walk around so I'm facing her again.

"You can open your eyes now."

She does, slowly, and looks down, reaching up with her hand to hold the necklace so she can see it better. She gasps. "Oh my god!" Her gaze flies to mine. "This is too much. After everything you've already done... this is too much."

"Nonsense. I want you to have it."

"But it must be worth a fortune." She shakes her head.

"So are you." I cup her face. I step closer, gaze never wavering.

"Nero, thank you for the best birthday ever. Not because of all the things you've given me, but because of you. You make me feel as if I'm worth something, and I haven't felt that way in a long time."

Cinder pushes up on her tiptoes and brings her mouth to mine. I don't know if she meant for it to be a chaste kiss or not, but the moment her lips touch mine, it devolves into something more primal.

My arms tug her close, and when I lick the seam of her lips, she opens for me, moaning into my mouth as our tongues slide together. Her hand pushes into my hair at the back of my head, and when my hard cock presses against the fabric of my pants, I slide my hand to her lower back and press her harder into me.

A needy sound slips out of her, and my willpower breaks, no longer able to hold back the instincts I've been denying. I need to know what she tastes like. I want to hear and watch her come when my face is pressed between her thighs.

I pull away from the kiss and smirk when I see the disappointment on her face. "Don't worry, princess, we're not done here. I have one last present to give you."

I bend and pick her up, carrying her over to the table we just dined upon. Time for my second dessert. She doesn't protest as I set her on her feet beside the table, then with one swipe of my arm, I send everything on the table crashing to the floor.

If Cinder's disturbed by my show of aggression, she doesn't show it.

I lift her by the waist, setting her on the edge of the table. "Lie down and spread your legs. I need to know what you taste like."

Her eyelids lower, and she does what I ask without argument.

"Princesses get rewarded, Cinder. Let me show you how." I push her legs further apart and move the fabric of her dress out of the way.

Seeing the expensive lingerie—a pale blue lace thong—wrapped around her pussy, knowing I provided it, makes me want to beat my chest like a fucking caveman. I rip the lace to shreds, discarding it behind me. Maybe I'll beat off with it around my cock later when I relive this moment.

Cinder looks at me with wide eyes, but there's no fear in them, so I drop to my knees and yank her hips toward me so that her pussy is front and center. Leaning in, I inhale deeply and kiss her inner thigh, groaning into her flesh at her sweet scent.

How the hell did I manage to resist for this long?

The first swipe of my tongue is like a hit of heroin—I'll be a slave to this addiction for life, always chasing the dragon.

I suck on her clit, and her hand slides through my hair. She tries to close her legs around my head, but I keep them pressed open with my hands.

She moans and grips my hair to the point of pain when I flick her clit several times then suck. Desperate to taste more of her, I move my attention to her entrance, fucking her with my tongue the way I want to with my cock. My balls are heavy and aching, but I ignore the desire to tug on myself. This is about Cinder and her pleasure.

Her musky sweet scent fills my mouth as she moves her hips.

That's right, princess, use me. Get your fill.

I move back up to her clit, bringing her close to coming before pulling her back from the edge. Her chest heaves as she tries to drag air into her lungs. Ready to bring her home, I push two fingers into her and curl them, moving them back and forth, then suck on her clit.

She explodes with a cry, gyrating her hips, and I use my free hand to keep her pressed to the table as she rides out her orgasm. She's panting on the table, dress hiked up with her legs splayed open as I lap up every last bit of her release. When I'm satisfied, I stand. She watches as I bring the two fingers that were inside her to my lips and suck on them.

Cinder licks her lips. She looks sated and as if she could fall asleep any minute. I reach down for her discarded panties and shove them in my pocket. Then I bend over the table and pick her up in my arms.

"C'mon. You've had a long day. Let's get you to bed."

She says nothing but leans her cheek into my chest as I walk through the manor to her bedroom. Once we're inside, I lay her on the bed and look down at her.

I'm about to help her dress for bed, but she gives me a sleepy smile, rolls onto her side, and drifts off to sleep. I don't have the heart to wake her, even if she's still wearing her dress.

After I turn off all the lights in the room, I sit in a chair in the corner and watch her sleep for longer than I'd admit to anyone.

Tonight has only increased my obsession with Cinder, not satiated it.

CHAPTER
SIXTEEN

CINDER

Two weeks have passed since my birthday and Nero has been keeping his distance from me once again—not eating with me, just saying a quick hello when he pokes his head in my room before I turn in for the night.

Was my birthday another regret of things he's done with me? I, for one, do not regret it. It was the single most thrilling and exciting moment of my life. I'd never had a man go down on me before, and I honestly didn't know that anything sexual could be *that good*.

If I didn't know better, I'd almost think it was a fever dream. But no, he's stoked something in me that continues to burn, even weeks later. Now we're back to Nero not touching me, barely talking to me, and I'm living in his house.

Since I worked late last night at Black Magic Bar, I get up late on Sunday morning. I'm getting used to this sleeping in thing now that I don't have to do a bunch of chores. I check the time and realize I only have an hour and a half before I have to be ready.

Anabelle tracked me down a few days ago and asked me if I wanted to spend today with her and Rapsody. It's probably silly, but I've never had any girlfriends before, at least outside of the places I work, and I'm a little nervous to spend a day with them. What if they don't like me once they get to really know me?

I put that worry aside and get out of bed, heading straight to the shower.

An hour and a half later, right on schedule, there's a knock on my door. Anabelle and Rapsody stand there, dressed casually.

"Hey. I wasn't sure what to wear. Is this okay?" I look down at my jeans and snug T-shirt.

"Perfect for what we're going to do," Anabelle says. "We're going bowling."

"Have you ever bowled before?" Rapsody asks. "I'm a first-timer."

"A few times when I was little. I didn't realize there was a bowling alley in Magnolia Bend."

Anabelle grins. "There's not. But there's one in Midnight Manor."

My mouth drops open. "No way!" What doesn't this place have?

We start down the dim hallway together, side by side, Rapsody giddy with excitement.

"This is our first time in the south wing. We had to have Nero draw us a map so we could find you," Anabelle says, laughing.

"Really? I assumed you would know every nook and cranny in this place."

She shakes her head. "No, the guys stay out of each other's wings if they can help it. I've never had any need to venture into Nero's private space until you arrived."

I smile at them and a tingling sensation travels up my spine, as though someone is watching me. I've had the same sensation more than a few times over the last month, and I still can't explain it. This place can be pretty creepy, especially at night. Though I usually feel pretty comfortable in the middle of the day.

"Can I ask you guys something?" I look between them as we pass by the stained-glass raven.

"Of course," Rapsody says.

"Do you guys ever get the feeling like you're being watched here?"

They share a look then return their attention to me.

"Strange things happen around here sometimes," Anabelle says, but she doesn't elaborate.

Anabelle leads us to a room and opens the doors. Of course it's not like any bowling alley I ever remember going to. It's elaborately decorated with arches and pillars separating the lanes.

"Asher said everything should be good to go. He asked Marcel to make sure before we got here, and someone will bring us drinks and snacks."

"Yay for girl time!" Rapsody says.

Excitement bubbles inside me like an overfilled glass of champagne. The idea that I might be able to build a friendship with these women feels like a novelty I never thought I'd have. After my dad married Louise, I had high hopes of having sisters close to my age to talk to and laugh with. But I was wrong on that front.

Fear surfaces quickly. What if Nero eventually asks me to leave Midnight Manor? Will this friendship survive?

"Let's do this," Anabelle says, taking a seat in front of the monitor and entering our names.

"I'm going to suck so bad," Rapsody says, though she doesn't sound that worried about it.

"I'm not going to be great either. It's been well over a decade since I've bowled." I try to make her feel better.

Rapsody picks up one of the bowling balls. "Wow. These are heavier than I thought."

She goes on to explain how sheltered she was when she was raised. I get the sense there's more to the story, but I don't want to pry when we're just getting to know each other.

"Okay, we're all set!" Anabelle says, popping up off the seat. "Cinder, I put you first, then Rapsody, then me."

I chuckle and walk toward the bowling balls and pick one

up. "Is that so Rapsody and I don't feel too bad when we see how good you are?"

"I'm going to be terrible, don't worry."

I take the ball to the line, trying to visualize what I want it to do, then I pull my arm back and release it. It starts off pretty well, but about halfway down, the ball veers left and ends up in the gutter. The girls cheer anyway, and I grab another ball. This time I manage to take out one pin on the end.

I shrug and return to where they are. "Better than nothing."

Rapsody goes next. We try to give her a few pointers, but both her balls end up in the gutter.

Then Anabelle takes her turn. She manages to knock down all but two pins.

We keep rotating through our turns, and at the end of the first game, Anabelle is the clear winner, with me having the second highest score, then Rapsody.

"Do you guys want to break for some food and drinks before we play the next game?" Rapsody asks. "I need to let the sting of defeat wear off."

Anabelle and I laugh.

"I'm getting hungry. I could definitely eat. I worked late at the bar last night, so I slept in and didn't have time to eat breakfast."

A member of the staff had come in and left us some food and drinks while we were in the middle of the game, so the three of us go over to the table and take a seat around it. There's an assortment of pub foods—nachos, wings, french fries, some veggies and ranch dip, and some mozzarella sticks.

"How's married life?" I ask Anabelle before biting a fry.

She gives me the widest smile. "Amazing. We're planning a trip to Europe in the coming months. I've never been and really want to go. Somehow, I convinced my reclusive husband to take me."

"That sounds amazing. Where all are you planning to go?" I dip another french fry in ketchup and eat it.

Anabelle tells us all about her plans, and I can't help but imagine myself doing the same thing with Nero. When she's done filling us in, I turn my attention to Rapsody.

"Any wedding plans underway yet?"

She shakes her head. "You don't know this, but years ago, Kol and I were engaged, though we never made it to the altar." She frowns. Seems my instincts were right that there's a lot more to her story. "That time we'd planned to get married at city hall, just the two of us. That's more our speed. Who knows, maybe we'll do that again."

"Don't you dare! If you do, you'd better make sure I'm there," Anabelle says.

Rapsody laughs. "Well, whatever we do, I don't think it will be a big affair."

"Fine." Anabelle rolls her eyes playfully then turns to look at me. "What about you?"

"I'm not getting married." A nervous laugh leaves my lips.

"But if you were to get married, what would you want your wedding to be like?" she asks.

"I used to think I'd want a huge affair with lots of people, flowers everywhere, and an expensive designer dress. Now..." I shrug. "I don't know. Now I think what matters is who's waiting at the end of the aisle."

"Amen to that," Anabelle says.

"Speaking of... can I ask what's going on with you and Nero?" Interest sparks in Rapsody's eyes.

My cheeks heat. I'm not sure how to answer. Will Nero be upset if I tell his brothers' significant others what we've done?

I can be truthful about one thing. "I'm really not sure. He's hot and cold."

They nod knowingly.

"It's the Voss way," Anabelle says with amusement in her tone.

My head tilts. "What do you mean?"

"Asher and Kol were the same. If you're into him, my advice is to just be patient. He'll figure himself out, and once he does, he'll be all in."

I don't want her words to give me false hope, but I can't help it. "You think?"

"Definitely," Rapsody says, sounding so sure.

"I don't know. Just when I think I'm making some headway with him, he disappears." I take a bite from a mozzarella stick.

"Like I said, it's the Voss way." Anabelle gives me a reassuring smile.

I hesitate to bring up something I've been wondering about, but it's been in the back of my head every time I'm around these women. "Did he tell you how we met?"

Rapsody shakes her head. "No, but I'm ready for the details."

I nervously laugh. "We met at the strip club where I work." Not entirely true, but it doesn't matter.

I watch their eyes for any signs of judgment but find none. I know for sure that Anabelle knows I work at T&T's, but I don't know about Rapsody. If she's surprised at all, she doesn't show it.

"For months he would come in and watch me dance from a table at the back and then leave before I was on the floor."

"Okay..." Anabelle waits for me to continue.

"I guess what I'm asking is, do you think Nero could ever fall for someone like me?"

Understanding blankets Anabelle's face, and she frowns. "You mean a beautiful, friendly, smart woman? Yes, I do."

I shift uncomfortably. "But he's a *Voss*. Could he really be with a stripper?"

Anabelle squeezes my hand. "Honey, you wouldn't be here if the answer was no."

I think about her words and realize she's probably right. Nero is letting me stay here in his home and has made no indication that he wants me to leave any time soon.

"We all have a past," Rapsody says. "It doesn't make any of us any less worthy."

I get the feeling she's speaking from personal experience, and I give them a small smile. "Thanks, ladies. I'll try to be patient then."

They both nod, and we keep eating.

I miss Nero. I haven't seen him since yesterday morning. A part of me hoped I'd find him waiting for me when I returned late last night after my shift, but no such luck.

Then I remember my shift last night at Black Magic Bar and the line of expensive vehicles that came through Magnolia Bend, heading to Midnight Manor. The same line of cars that rolls through town on the last Saturday of every month.

I remember the first Saturday night I worked there and saw them and asked one of the locals what it was all about. They said no one knows. Apparently, the cars have come for decades, but no one knows who or what they're here for. Urban legend claims there's some kind of ritualistic sacrifice that happens once a month, and others claim it's a meeting of the Illuminati. I didn't hear anything last night.

I decide I'm going to ask the girls to get a straight answer. "I was working the bar last night and couldn't help but notice all the vehicles that came through town on their way here. What's that about?"

Anabelle stops bringing her mozzarella stick to her mouth, her eyes pinging to Rapsody, who swallows and gives me an expression to say she definitely knows what I'm talking about. The space fills with an uncomfortable tension. I shouldn't have asked.

I wave them off. "It's okay, you don't have to tell me."

Anabelle's shoulders sag. "We wish we could, but we can't. I'm sorry. If we could tell you, we would. But maybe ask Nero."

I nod. "Okay, no biggie."

Are the townspeople right in their assumptions? I don't know what I just walked into, but it's clear it was the wrong thing to ask. One thing is for sure, Midnight Manor has its own secrets.

CHAPTER
SEVENTEEN

CINDER

I plop down in my seat in the changing room at T&T's, ready to wipe off my makeup, and my stomach rumbles something fierce.

"You'd better feed that thing," Trina says, walking past.

I chuckle and pick up a makeup wipe, but my phone rings from inside my locker, so I set it down and get up to answer. It's not often that my phone rings—I don't know that many people.

When I look at the screen, it's Lisa.

"Hey, girl, shouldn't you be in here already?" I ask, knowing she has the night shift while I worked this afternoon.

"Cinder, I'm so sorry, but I'm desperate."

I straighten. "What's wrong?"

"My sister was supposed to watch the kids, but she went on a bender today. There's no way she can drive here to the motel, let alone watch the kids."

"What can I do to help?" I pull my street clothes out of my locker.

"Is there any chance you can come watch the kids while I work? They'll only be awake for another few hours, and then you can just watch TV until I get back."

"Of course. I'll leave now. Just text me the address."

She sighs with relief. "Thank you, you're a lifesaver. I owe you."

"Don't worry about it. I'm happy to. I'll see you soon." I end the call and shove my phone in my locker while I quickly get changed. I don't bother removing my makeup. I'll do it at the motel.

My phone dings with a text. Must be Lisa giving me the address. But then it dings a second time.

Once I'm changed, I grab all my stuff from my locker and rush out the back door to my vehicle, waving at Aiyden over my shoulder.

When I'm seated in the car, I pull out my phone and see a text from Lisa and one from my stepmother. I ignore Louise's text demanding to know where I am as I've done for a month straight. After mapping out the motel's location, I drive away from T&T's.

I'm disappointed there's no chance I'll see Nero tonight since I won't be home until really late. He was here earlier to watch me dance, and as always, he left before I came out onto the floor.

A few days have passed since I bowled with Anabelle and Rapsody, and I've decided to take their advice and just be patient with Nero and hope that they're right. If that doesn't work, I'll figure something else out, but I've been able to save some money at least by staying there and not having to give everything to Louise and my wicked step-sisters.

I arrive at the motel and park my car, then rush to room number three, knocking on the door.

Lisa whips open the door. "Thank you so much!"

She hurriedly waves me in, and I step inside to find two little girls sitting on one of the two beds, wide-eyed and staring at me. I know from Lisa that they're six and four years old.

"Hi, girls!" I smile and wave, but they just look at me nervously.

Poor things. I'm not quite sure that they've been privy to the dynamic between their parents, but if I had to guess, I'd say they've seen some shit.

"Dahlia and Rose, this is my friend from work, Cinder. She's going to keep an eye on you while I work since Aunt Sheila isn't feeling well, okay? You be good girls for her." Lisa gives them both a quick kiss and a hug.

"We're going to have fun, aren't we, girls?" I give them a big smile, but neither of them says anything. Tough crowd.

Lisa hugs me. "Be back as soon as I can. Thank you."

"We'll be fine. See you in a while."

Lisa walks out, and I lock the door behind her. I turn around and survey the motel room. It's dated, with condensation rings on all the furniture from drinks left on it over the years. The bedding looks as if it's probably about forty years old, and a faint musty odor permeates everything.

I can't believe they've been living like this for months. This is no place for these girls to grow up, though it's better than watching their father abuse their mother. I have to figure out some way I can help them get somewhere better.

These sweet girls are obviously a little wary of me, so I sit on the other bed and turn my attention to the TV. "What are you girls watching?"

Neither of them answers me. I don't want to push them, so I arrange a pillow that feels as if it's no thicker than a piece of cardboard behind me and lean against the headboard to watch. After about ten minutes, one of them asks me a question.

"Are you a dancer like my mommy?"

Dahlia, the oldest, is looking at me, and that's when I remember that I still have my makeup on. Lisa has told me that her girls know she's a dancer but have no idea what she really does.

"I am."

"Your makeup is pretty," she says.

I smile. "Thank you. Do you like to dance?"

She frowns, and her eyes grow sadder. "I don't know how."

Finally, some common ground and a way to have fun with them. "If you want, I can teach you something. I started taking dance classes when I was really little."

A spark of happiness grows in her eyes. "Okay!"

I look at Rose, whose attention is still fixed on the TV. "Do you think Rose would like to learn something too?"

Dahlia looks at her and shakes her head. "She's too shy."

"Okay, no problem. If she wants to join in, she can just let us know, how does that sound?"

Dahlia nods excitedly and slides off the bed, as do I. I walk over to where there's a small amount of room at the end of the beds. It's not a lot, but we'll make it work.

"Okay, the first thing I'm going to teach you is a step-ball-change. The first thing you need to do is to step out to the side with this foot." I motion to her right side.

She does as I ask. "Like that?"

"Perfect. Okay, now take your other foot and put it behind that foot."

She tries to do it but seems a little confused.

"May I touch your leg and show you?" Dahlia nods, so I crouch down in front of her, placing my hand on her right leg. "Put all your weight on this leg, and then move this one." I reach for her left ankle and show her where to move it and set it behind her right leg. "Just like that, great!"

She wobbles and stumbles to the side as I stand up.

"That's okay, it takes practice to balance like that. That's something you can work on." I smile, and she seems reassured by my words, which knits together something in my chest. "Just put your legs back how they were."

She does as I ask.

I glance at Rose on the bed. She's watching us with interest, rather than the TV.

"Okay, now your foot is at the back. See if you can put all your weight on that foot, but try to keep it on this part." I lift my foot and point at the ball of my foot.

Dahlia shifts her weight and wobbles, sticking her arms out to the sides to balance herself.

"Good. Now lift your front foot and put it back down." She does, and I clap. "You did it! That's a step-ball-change."

"Yay!" She jumps up and down and claps for herself.

I could cry from witnessing the transformation in her demeanor from when I first entered this room. It fills me with such joy.

"When you get used to the movements and do it a little faster, keeping your balance will be a lot easier," I tell her.

Dahlia tries it again, messes up, starts over and is able to get through the whole movement.

Once she's bored of that move, I teach her a box step and a jazz walk, all while Rose watches quietly from the bed.

I'm being silly, and the two of us are laughing when the pounding starts on the door. We both startle, and Rose makes a strangled cry from the bed, pulling her legs up to her chest.

"Lisa, you fucking bitch, you'd better open this goddamned door before I kick it down! I'm tired of this shit!"

He pounds again, and I spring into action, gripping Dahlia's shoulders and hunching down so we're at eye level.

"See this here?" I point at the deadbolt lock on the door. "When I go out and talk to your daddy, do you think you can flip it back this way as soon as the door closes?"

She bites her lip, tears in her eyes, and nods. "Daddy's mad," she whispers, and my heart breaks.

"I'm going to try to calm him down. As soon as the door closes, you flip that lock, okay? And you don't open it for anyone except me, okay?"

More pounding and cursing erupt from him.

She nods again.

I pull her in and give her a hug. "It's okay. It's going to be okay. After you've locked the door, I want you to take Rose and go into the bathroom and lock the door. I'll shout for you to open the door for me once everything's calmed down."

I have experience dealing with drunks at Black Magic Bar and guys who can be too handsy at T&T's, but my hands shake as I straighten and grip the door handle.

"Open up this fucking door!"

I look over my shoulder at Dahlia. "Ready?"

She nods, lips quivering as I unlock the door and push my way out of the room, quickly shutting the door behind me. I hear the deadbolt click into place. *Good girl.*

"Who the hell are you?" The man steps back and gives me the once-over.

He has on a dirty flannel shirt, splayed open to reveal a stained white T-shirt underneath. I don't think he's had a shower in days. Based on the smell of him, he's been drinking.

"You must be one of Lisa's whore friends from the club. Where the fuck is she?" He makes for the door, and I remain where I am, pushing at his chest.

"She's not here. You should go. You're scaring your daughters."

He scowls. "That fucking slut thinks she can take my kids from me. Thinks she's too good for me. I'll show her!"

He tries to push his way around me again, and this time I push harder, standing my ground.

"You tryin' to come between me and my girls? Bitch, you don't wanna do that." He grips my upper arm hard, and I cry out.

"Just leave. I'll tell Lisa you came by, and she can call you when she gets back."

He squeezes harder, and I wince, my knees buckling. "She busy whoring herself out, that it? That why you're here watching my kids, and they're not with me?" He moves me to the side and slams me against the wall, raising his fist.

I brace myself, knowing he's never shied away from hitting Lisa, the woman he supposedly loves. I'm just some woman he doesn't know or care about. But before his fist lands on my face, he's tackled onto the concrete by Nero.

What the hell is he doing here?

CHAPTER
EIGHTEEN

NERO

I watch from my vehicle as Cinder knocks on the motel room door.

What the hell is she doing at this dive motel on the county line? Is she meeting someone? My hands grip the steering wheel even tighter with the thought that she's been playing me.

Thankfully, I don't lose my shit and storm out of my car because the woman who opens the door is someone I recognize. She's one of the other dancers at T&T's. Maybe Cinder's just visiting a friend? Though she's never come here after any of her shifts at T&T's before. She usually goes to Black Magic Bar or Midnight Manor.

Continuing to watch the room, I see the other woman leave a few minutes later, but Cinder remains inside. I settle in, wondering what she's doing and why she's staying when her friend is leaving. Cinder hasn't moved her things out of

Midnight Manor. I've given the staff strict instructions to let me know when they go in to clean her room daily.

Maybe she decided to leave the manor, leaving all her stuff behind, because of how on and off I've been. I ate her out on her birthday then ignored her for weeks. She probably doesn't know what to make of me or what I want.

But she's never mentioned what happened—either at T&T's or on her birthday. She's never pushed me to explain myself. Almost as though she understands that I need time to get my head on straight. Though try as I might, it still feels inevitable that something between us is going to break. It's like we're barrelling down the tracks, a runaway train with no brakes, and at some point, we're going to collide. The question is, what will the damage be afterward?

I can't get this woman out of my system, and I fear that if I give all of myself to her, I might become more obsessed than ever. But it's becoming harder and harder to control my urge to claim her.

I watch for another hour, but it's getting late, and I'm tired. Between watching Cinder all the time and trying to keep up with things at Voss Enterprises, sleep is a rarity these days.

I must drift off, but I'm woken by shouting. I bolt up and look at room three. Cinder and a man are standing in front of the door, the man screaming at her.

What the fuck?

I bolt out of the car and run toward the room, seeing the sleazebag with his hand on Cinder's arm, pushing her against the brick wall.

This motherfucker must have a death wish.

I plow him over, both of us falling to the ground, me on top of him. Cinder yelps, but all I can think of is making this guy pay for putting his hands on Cinder.

He fights, wiggling under me, but I throw a leg over and straddle him. My fists hit him over and over. He tries to get a punch in on me from below, but I dodge it.

"How dare you lay your filthy fucking hands on her." I punch him in the face right where blood is already trickling down his cheek. He groans. "I ought to slice you open and rip out your insides, you piece of shit." I hit him again, the crack of cartilage echoing in the darkness. Blood splatters all over me.

"Nero!" Cinder's hands wrap around my bicep.

I look at her over my shoulder, and her eyes are wide and full of fear.

Fear of *me*?

You'd think I'd beat the shit out of myself from the worthless feeling inside me.

I look down at the asshole. He groans, holding his hand to his nose. He's not fighting back anymore. My chest heaves, but I'm satisfied he's not an immediate threat to Cinder. I get off him.

"Are you okay?" I clutch her shoulders, looking her up and down. She's not bleeding, so that's a good sign.

She nods, her eyes falling to the bastard, her face still stricken with fear.

"Is he your ex? Is that why you were trying to get me off him?"

Her gaze picks up, staring at me. "No. His kids are inside, and they're scared."

The boiling anger dissipates. Now the situation makes sense. She's watching her friend's kids, and this guy is obviously tied to her friend.

I turn back around and stand over him. "Get the hell out of here and don't think of coming back. Understood?"

He glares at me, wincing when he touches his broken nose. "I should fucking sue you for breaking my nose."

I scoff. "I'd like to see you try. Now get the fuck out of here and don't come back." I bend down and grab the front of his shirt, yanking him to his feet. "Go."

I shove him toward the parking lot. He stumbles, looks as if he wants to say more, but wisely turns and staggers off toward an old pickup. It doesn't turn over right away, but eventually the starter catches, and the engine roars to life. As he drives away, he flips us off, screaming something I can't hear.

Now that he's gone, I give Cinder my undivided attention. "Are you sure you're not hurt?"

"Just shaken." She turns and knocks on the motel room door. "Dahlia, it's Cinder. Everything is okay now. Can you open the door?"

There's no sound or movement from behind the door.

Her shoulders sag, then she looks at me with tears in her eyes and whispers, "They're probably so scared." She

164

knocks again. "Dahlia, it's okay. He's gone, and everything is fine. Can you open the door please, sweetie?"

We wait for thirty seconds before we hear movement behind the cheap door, then the sound of a deadbolt turning, and the door cracks open an inch.

Cinder sighs in relief. "Are you and Rose okay?"

The door opens a little more, and a little girl with mousy brown hair stands there in her PJs. Her eyes widen when she spots me.

"It's okay, it's okay. This is my friend, Nero." Cinder puts her hand on my arm.

I smile and hold up a hand in a wave, then crouch down to her height. "Hi, Dahlia. I'm one of Cinder's good friends. Would it be okay if I came and hung out with you guys until your mom gets back?"

Her gaze darts between Cinder and me before she nods.

We go in the room, and Dahlia scurries to the far bed and tucks herself under the covers as if the thin bedspread is a protective barrier from all the shit going on in her life. Cinder heads toward the bathroom and comes out holding the hand of a younger girl who resembles her sister. She scurries up on the bed to sit beside Dahlia.

"Rose, this is my friend, Nero. He's going to hang out with us until your mom gets back just in case there's any more trouble, okay?"

Rose nods.

Cinder walks over to me, bringing me by the hand over to the corner of the room.

"I need to call Lisa and tell her what happened just in case he shows up at work," she says in a low voice. "Can you stay out here while I make the call in the bathroom?"

I nod.

She looks back at the girls. "I'm just going to make a quick call in the bathroom. Be right back." Her voice holds false cheer that I'm sure the girls see through, but I still admire how Cinder's handling the situation.

Not a surprise. This woman always amazes me.

While she's in the bathroom, I send a few texts. A few minutes later, the bathroom door opens, and Cinder comes out.

"Good news! Your mom is on her way back."

Both girls nod, though they're holding one another's hands, not ready to let go.

The four of us sit in silence, watching a kid's show that makes me want to gouge out my eyeballs. Seriously, it's painful.

A half hour later, a knock sounds on the door. I put my hand up to stop Cinder from approaching, and I go to the door and look through the peephole.

"It's me," says a woman from the other side of the door.

Sure enough, it's the woman who left a while back. I unlock the deadbolt and swing the door open. Lisa, as I now know her, rushes in but stops when she sees me.

"This is my friend, Nero," Cinder says. "He helped calm things down."

I'm not sure I'd put it that way, but hey, whatever.

Lisa nods and continues straight to her daughters. She wraps her arms around them both. "Are you girls okay?"

Their little hands grip their mom as though they're afraid she might disappear, and the youngest sobs into her mom's chest.

My chest squeezes, and my hand rubs over my heart to relieve the ache. I was once like that little girl.

Pushing that thought out of my mind, I clear my throat. "I arranged for you to stay somewhere else. Wrote the information down on the notepad." I gesture to the small, scarred table in the corner. "It's a little farther out from"—I glance at the two small girls—"your work, but there's security, and no one gets in or out unless they're a guest."

Lisa watches me as though maybe I'm the predator, then her eyes flicker to Cinder with a questioning expression. She untangles herself from her daughters and walks over to the table, picking up the notepad.

"I can't afford this place." She drops the notepad back on the table.

"You don't have to. My family owns it. You can stay there as long as you need to, free of charge."

Cinder's gaze bores into the side of my head, but I don't look over. No, I shift uncomfortably on my feet because I'm not used to being the one who swoops in like the superhero. I'm more the villain type the superhero is trying to save people from.

Lisa looks between Cinder and me a couple of times, then seems to realize her best bet here is to say thank you and not look a gift horse in the mouth. Good. If I had to work to convince her my motives were true, I might just tell her to forget the whole fucking thing.

"Thank you," she says. "That's really nice of you."

"Can we help you pack up?" Cinder asks.

"There's not much, but yeah. That'd be great. I want to get out of here in case Freddie decides to return."

Once we've packed up Lisa and her girls' meager belongings and put them in her vehicle with the girls, Cinder and I watch them drive off into the night.

Cinder turns to me under the stark one light in the parking lot. "That was a really nice thing for you to do."

I shove my hands in my pockets. "No child should have to grow up around violence." I don't look at her, but I feel her eyes on me.

We're both silent for a beat.

"I guess I'll drive home now. My car is just parked over there." She gestures with her hand.

"Leave it. You're riding home with me. One of the staff will pick it up."

She doesn't argue and walks toward my vehicle, getting in as I said, and the fucked up part of me purrs from her doing my bidding.

Her eyes are on me as I start the car.

I look over. "What?"

168

Her blue eyes are wide. "Nero, what were you doing here when Freddie showed up? Why were you here?"

Fuck, with all the crap going on, I forgot she would question why I was in the parking lot of a dingy motel. I'm going to have to come clean with her. But I'm starting to think that maybe the obsessive, domineering side of me is about keeping her safe and protecting her, not about controlling her everyday life—we'll save that for the bedroom.

CHAPTER
NINETEEN

CINDER

"Nero, what were you doing here when Freddie showed up? Why were you here?"

At first, he doesn't appear as if he's going to answer me. He shifts the car into drive and leaves the parking lot. But I hope he's not ignoring my questions, and he's just framing his response.

"I don't even know where to start." He frowns at the dark road ahead, not glancing at me.

"The beginning is usually a good place."

He nods, and a deep sigh slips from his lips. "My father was an asshole. That's putting it mildly, I guess. He was a lot like Freddie was tonight, only his money and prestige protected him. Used to knock my mother around, beat my brothers and me. Did other deplorable things I'm not going to haunt you with. Pretty much made our lives hell until he died."

My throat tightens. "Was... was he the one who murdered your mother?"

Nero shakes his head and something passes over his face but the emotion is so quick—there and then gone—that I have no time to make sense of it. "No. She had an affair with another man, and when she wouldn't leave my father, he murdered her. Stabbed her in the heart with a pair of gardening shears right in the garden. She loved that garden..."

I wish we were already back at the manor so that I could wrap him in my arms and hold him for as long as he'd let me. If he'd let me.

Though I didn't spend the last decade in the best of situations, what Nero endured sounds far worse than anything I can fathom.

I place my hand over his resting on the stick shift. "I'm so sorry. No child should have to deal with that."

He doesn't look at me, keeping his eyes on the road, but he nods. "That's why I moved your friend and her girls. They shouldn't have to worry about him showing up again. They're probably already traumatized by whatever they've seen, never mind what went down tonight."

Nero seems to always be protecting everyone. First me, and now Lisa and the girls. "Thank you for doing that."

He nods again.

"But it doesn't explain what you were doing there."

His hands tighten on the steering wheel. "No, it doesn't."

He gulps. "I told you that my mom died when I was six, and my father, thank God, died when I was twelve."

My chest squeezes at all the loss he endured as a child. I know firsthand how it shapes you. "Was your dad sick?"

He takes a quick glance at me and shakes his head. "No."

Nero offers no more information. It's clear that even if I pry, he won't fill me in.

"Anyway, after my dad died, though I wasn't heartbroken in the least, it still fucked with me. I didn't have anyone other than my brothers, and I realized that I'd never known a parent's love. I started... fixating on people. I don't really know why. If I went to a psychologist, I'm sure they could tell me, but by the time I was in the middle of high school, it ramped up. I met this girl... Farrah MacIntyre."

My forehead wrinkles. "That name sounds familiar."

He nods. "You probably know of her father, Senator MacIntyre."

My eyes widen. He's always in the news, and it was thought that in the next election, he'd be one of the front-runners for the party's nomination for president.

"We met and became friends, and I was into her but never pursued it because I..." He glances at me before staring back at the road. "I got off on stalking her."

The words rush out of him, and I piece them together in my head.

My eyes widen, and I pull my hand away, linking my hands in my lap. "What exactly does that mean?"

173

The corners of his mouth tighten. "I'd watch her. Incessantly. She had no idea."

"Is that what you were doing with me? Is that why you were in the motel parking lot tonight?"

"Yes." His voice is a pained whisper. "But I set boundaries. I never followed you home."

My head rocks back as thoughts swirl through my head, chasing each other. Thankfully he never did find out where I lived because then he'd know that I was Maude's stepsister. The coating of guilt on my skin thickens even more. I should tell him who Maude is to me. But somehow fear makes the words die on my tongue.

"I've been watching you from afar since the first night I saw you dance." There's shame in his tone, and though I want to comfort him, I don't.

"Why me?"

He turns onto a desolate country road, the only light around us is his headlights shining ahead. "I honestly don't know. There was just something about you and the way you danced that drew me in. I couldn't get enough of you."

I frown. "But you never stayed after my dance. You'd watch and leave."

He nods. "I was trying to keep myself in check. I was becoming more and more obsessed with you, and that's why I only allowed myself to watch you dance, and I'd force myself to leave. Until that night in the VIP..."

I shift in my seat, thinking about the way he knew what to

do to my body to take me to heights I've never reached before.

"After that, my obsession with you grew, so I stayed away. Until I saw you leave the bar that night and invited you to stay at Midnight Manor."

I glance away from him at the mention of that night and change the subject. "And my birthday... why did you stay away after?"

He sighs, and I turn to him. "Same reason."

"What happens if your obsession becomes too much for you?" I ask in a soft voice.

"I don't know, but I fear it will be similar to what happened in high school."

My stomach pitches. "Which was?"

Nero swallows hard. "My stalking escalated. Soon I was breaking into her house when she wasn't there to go through her bedroom. I started leaving her anonymous notes. I'd watch her while she slept. One night I was watching from outside, and she snuck a guy into her room. I lost it. As though she was cheating on me when we had no commitment to each other except the one in my head. I'd convinced myself she liked my attention. I crawled in through her window and attacked him. You can imagine the fallout.

"When I saw how terrified Farrah was when she heard about the extent of my stalking and that I had been the one leaving her the notes, watching her sleep—I've never been so ashamed. My brothers bailed me out. To this day, the Voss family is still one of Senator MacIntyre's biggest campaign contributors. After everything went down, I promised my brothers it wouldn't happen again, and after all they did to protect me from our father when I was younger, I owed them that. And I stuck to it." He turns his head to meet my gaze. "Until you."

So many emotions are whirling through my chest like a tornado. "Pull over."

His head whips to look at me again. "What?"

"Pull. Over."

He pulls to the side of the dark country road, leaving us surrounded by empty fields.

I put my hand on the door latch.

"Cinder, I'm not going to hurt you. I'll take you wherever you want to go, but I'm not leaving you in the middle of nowhere."

"Get out." I push open my door. When he doesn't move, I glare at him. "Get out."

I exit the vehicle, and he crawls out as if he's worried what the fallout will be from his admission.

I walk to the front of the vehicle and pace, stepping through the beam of the headlights over and over again, trying to make sense of what I'm feeling and thinking.

A logical person would probably be frightened by every-thing he just told me, but... I'm not. In some weird, fucked up way, I feel almost... flattered. Flattered because he fixated and spied on me for months. Flattered that he chose me. Flattered that maybe he feels the same as I do.

Nero watches me pace and doesn't say a word.

I hate that he's probably assuming I'm afraid of him or questioning my feelings for him when nothing could be further from the truth. My feet come to a stop, and I meet his gaze through the dark.

The pull between us is still there, stronger than ever, like a rope strung between his heart and mine, growing tighter and tighter, pulling me in.

The cool night air brushes against my skin as I walk toward him. His eyes are full of fear over what I might say. When I reach him, I wrap my arms around him and squeeze tightly.

He circles his arms around my waist, lowers his head into my hair, and breathes me in.

"I'm sorry you had to go through all of that at such a young age."

Nero's body relaxes in my arms, and he tucks me into his big frame.

This man doesn't scare me. In fact, I've never felt safer or more protected. It's clear to me that no part of Nero wants to hurt me, obsession or not. He only wants what's best for me and to protect me.

I pull away from him and look into his eyes. The blue is like a stormy sea in the darkness of the ocean rather than the bright blue of a sunny day.

"I'm not afraid of you, Nero." I cradle his cheek in my palm. "I'm not afraid of your desire to watch me. I'm not concerned whether you are or aren't obsessed with me. None of that matters."

Relief lands on his face, and he pushes his hands into my hair, bringing his lips to mine. He lets me in. Letting me see all the parts that make him who he is.

Our tongues meet with fervor, our hands gripping and clawing at each other. One minute we're standing in front of each other, and the next his hands are grabbing my ass and placing me on the hood of his luxury car. His hands slide up my inner thighs, inching them open until he stands between my legs. He tugs me closer, and his arousal presses against the seam of my jeans. I moan as his hand traces a path over my shirt, gripping my breast.

I've never felt this needy for a man in my life. As though I'll die if I don't have him.

I work the button and zipper of his pants, my hand sliding down the waistband of his boxer briefs and wrapping my hand around his length. He growls into my mouth, pumping his hips firmly. God, he's big. Bigger than any man I've ever been with.

With his hand on the back of my head, he lowers me so my back is splayed over the front of the car. He furiously works on getting my shoes off, and I undo the button of my jeans, sliding down the zipper. Nero's hands pull frantically at the fabric, tugging the denim down my legs.

He tosses my jeans to the ground and tears off my thong. With his hands on my hips, he pulls me toward him so my ass hangs on the edge of the hood. He fists his cock and runs the tip through the wetness of my folds, teasing me.

"I need you, Nero." I heave out a breath, my orgasm at the brink, and he hasn't even entered me yet.

He lines up his dick, and slides into me. After a few thrusts of his hips, he's fully seated inside me. He stretches me, and I cry out.

The sex is hard and fast, desperate and feral. He pounds into me, and I take him, clawing at the car, needing anything to hold on to. Nero's hands are on my hips, keeping me stable, and my hands come to my breasts, squeezing and pinching my nipples since I can't reach him.

"Fuck, Cinder, you're so tight. So fucking perfect. I knew you would be." He tilts his head up, eyes closed as he fucks me hard and fast.

I can't get enough of this or him.

He brings one thumb to my clit, massaging it in a circle. It only takes seconds before I'm hit with a freight train of an orgasm, obliterated, shattering into pieces and floating out into the night like fragments of stardust.

Seconds later, Nero pulls out and comes on my mound with a groan. Breathing heavily, I watch him, knowing this visual will be locked in my brain for life.

I quickly realize that we were so caught up in one another we didn't use protection. I'm on birth control, so pregnancy isn't a concern, and I'm not worried about an STD on my part since I haven't had sex since the last time I was tested. But Nero, I don't know.

Nero stares at his seed coating me with a gleam in his eye.

"I'm on birth control," I blurt.

His eyes meet my gaze, and he smiles. "That's why I pulled out, but that's not why I'm looking. I like seeing my come on you." His fingers run down, coating the come all over my stomach and pussy. "Let's not wipe it off before you get dressed. We can shower when we get back to Midnight Manor."

"Okay. And I don't have any STDs either, just so you know."

He places his hands on either side of my shoulder, bending down and kissing me. "Me either."

I relax under him. "Good."

"But now that I know you're on birth control, the next time I fuck you, I'm going to come in your pussy."

I press my thighs together to release the ache. Inching up from the hood, I kiss him thoroughly. The kiss draws to a close, and he bends down, grabbing my underwear from the ground.

"Can't put these back on, but here are your pants."

He shoves my panties in his pocket. Now he's got two pairs of my panties. The other one came from the night of my birthday.

After grabbing my jeans, he helps me get them on then hands me my shoes, looking at the dark surrounding us. "We should get out of here before someone finds us."

"Right." I round the car and slide into the passenger side of the car, worried that maybe he's going to revert to his usual ways and push me away now that we've slept together.

"This is my favorite car." He rubs the top of the dash in front of him then looks at me. "Even more so now." He winks and puts the car in drive, speeding off into the night.

God, I'm not sure I could handle it if he did another disappearing act now.

CHAPTER
TWENTY

NERO

I t's all I can do not to pull the car over again on the way back to the manor and drag Cinder over the stick shift to ride me. The moment I sank into her, I was lost. I will never get enough of her. Ever.

Now that she knows everything, I feel lighter. Well, almost everything. I confessed my deepest shame, and she didn't send me packing. Surprisingly, she pulled me closer.

I park in front of the manor, and we climb out. The mansion has an even more ominous feeling to it in the dark. Heavy mist hangs low to the ground, and the low lights on the outside flicker in the darkness.

Cinder takes my hand, and I'm not sure if it's to stay connected with me or whether she's scared. I grew up here, so not much fazes me anymore, but sometimes Midnight Manor feels like an entity of its own.

We make our way through the manor to the south wing. I lead her to the en suite of my bedroom and start the shower to allow the water to heat up. She watches me with keen eyes, and I reach behind my neck, pulling my Henley over my head.

Her gaze darts to the large raven tattoo covering the side of my ribcage. Cinder breaks the distance, tracing her finger over one open wing, then over the large claws on the bird's feet.

Her gaze flicks to mine. "The stained glass and a tattoo. What does the raven mean?"

I wrap my hand around hers and bring it to my mouth, kissing her palm. "My mother used to call me her little raven because I had a good memory despite being young and was smart. She used to say I was wise beyond my years. Even though I was so little, I always wanted to protect her from my father." I swallow. "It's one of the few really solid memories I have of my mom."

Cinder runs her palm over my face. "You miss her."

I nod, my hands inching down to the hem of her shirt, pulling it up. Her hand leaves my cheek, allowing me to strip it off her.

"Yeah, though sometimes I think I'm missing a ghost. I don't remember enough to really miss *her* if that makes sense." I step closer to her, reach around to unhook her bra, and slide the straps down her arms.

Her bare tits are heavy on her chest, and as always, my hands itch to feel the weight of them. I remind myself that this time I don't have to hold back or control myself to not overstep. My hands cover her voluptuous tits, so much more than a handful, and I squeeze gently. Her eyes flutter closed.

I knead and rub, running my thumbs over her stiffened nipples, eliciting a soft moan from her. If I don't stop fixating on her tits, we won't make it into the shower.

I finish undressing her with her watching me, our eyes catching after each piece of disposed garment. Then I strip down, grab her hand, and lead her into the oversized walk-in shower with a showerhead on each end.

The water is hot and soothing, steam rising from the droplets of water filling the space. She drops her head back into the spray, moaning as the water coasts over her body. I watch the rivulets stream down her tits and drop off her nipples, my tongue aching to follow the same path.

"Let me shampoo your hair."

She smiles and turns around. I grab the shampoo bottle and empty a healthy dose into my palm, then massage it into her hair.

"That feels so good," she says as I run my fingertips over her scalp, working the shampoo into a lather.

My dick twitches between our bodies, but I ignore its desperate plea for attention, wanting to make this about her. I work the lather through her hair all the way down to the ends and guide her under the water so the back of her head is facing the spray again. While she washes the suds from her hair, I grab the conditioner and squirt it in my palm.

I look up to find Cinder looking at me, and her eyes are filled with lust. Her head is probably swimming with all the same naughty thoughts as mine, but I persevere and twirl my finger, instructing her to turn back around. I work the conditioner through her hair, finger-combing her long blonde strands, until it's all covered. I pull the showerhead from the wall and rinse it out myself.

When I finish, she circles around. "My turn."

She grabs the shampoo off the shelf, her nipples grazing my hard chest. My dick twitches between us, and she chuckles. I stifle a groan when she steps closer and brings her hands into my hair to massage the shampoo in. She intently watches what she's doing while I study her face.

She's so fucking beautiful. Those big blue eyes of hers are full of innocence, but her plump lips and the way they curve up at the corners is all sensuality. Unable to hold back any longer, I wrap my arms around her waist, pulling her in for a kiss, but I inadvertently step back into the spray, and the suds wash down my face and fill our mouths with a god-awful taste.

We both laugh, and I drag her into the spray with me until the shampoo washes away. Then I pick up the bar of soap.

"Ready to wash up now?" I arch an eyebrow.

Cinder bites her lower lip, and holy fuck, am I ever looking forward to seeing those lips wrapped around my cock.

"Why do I feel like I'm going to end up more dirty than clean?" she says with a smirk.

"Only one way to find out."

I start off innocently enough, rubbing the bar of soap over her back and her arms. Then I get down on my haunches and run the bar up and down her legs, over her amazing ass. Her breath hitches when it coasts over her mound and between her legs. After turning her toward the spray to rinse off, I stand. Once there's no more soap on her, she moves to step back out of the spray, but I cage her in from behind, forcing her chest into the tile.

My hand traces down her side, squeezing her ass before slipping between her folds. Cinder's forehead drops to the tile.

"Are you too sore for this?"

She shakes her head against the wall and arches her back, offering herself to me. I chuckle deep in my throat and push two fingers into her. When I scissor them, she moans, her hands forming fists against the wall.

My balls tighten with the urge to sink into her from behind and take her like a rutting animal, but I deny myself. This is about her realizing how good I can make her feel so that she's as obsessed with me as I am with her.

I pull them out of her slick heat, pushing them in again and again, picking up my pace until she's panting against the wall. When I wrap my other arm around her and fondle her swollen clit, she cries out. I suck on the curve of her neck until she's almost there, and when she reaches her highest point, I bite her flesh. She clenches around my fingers and comes on a cry, jutting her hips back and forth.

I let her ride out her orgasm and lick the place I just bit, mumbling into her skin, "If I wasn't already obsessed with you, tonight would do it."

187

She rests her cheek on the tile wall, looking at me over her shoulder. "The feeling is mutual."

The steady buzzing in my veins is tempered only by the knowledge that there's more I have to tell her. But how much can I pile on before her faith in me falters under the weight of my omissions? Tonight is not the night. She's already had to deal with enough, and even Cinder's understanding only goes so far. I still have a couple weeks before I'll have to tell her. I'm going to make them count.

CHAPTER
TWENTY-ONE

CINDER

I arrive back at the manor after my shift at Black Magic Bar, exhausted. I worked a double because the day-shift bartender called in sick. I'd like to spend some time with Nero, but physically, I need to sleep.

We slept together for the first time a week ago, and though I have no idea what our official status is, we've spent all our time in the manor fucking like rabbits everywhere and anywhere.

I can't get enough of him. Each time we're together, I think, "This is the time I'll feel satiated" but it never happens.

So rather than go in search of him, I text him that I'm exhausted and going straight to bed. After a quick shower, I put on my pajamas and slip under the covers, drifting to sleep right away.

Not long later, I'm awoken by a woman's voice calling my name over and over.

Blinking several times, I open my eyes and find myself already out of bed and walking out my bedroom door. Mist surrounding me blocks my sight of what's around me, but I'm familiar enough with the manor that I know I'm making my way through it. The same way you know things when you're having a dream, even if they're not there in front of you.

Wait—is this a dream?

The woman's voice says my name again, and I continue walking forward, almost not of my own volition. I feel as if I'm in a trance—aware of my surroundings, but unable to break free. I couldn't stop walking if I wanted to.

I drift through the mist, and it swirls around me until I arrive at a large intricately carved wooden door. My hand reaches out to turn the handle, but it's locked. I try again, and that's when my name comes from behind me.

Only this time, it's not a woman's voice saying it.

"Cinder, what are you doing?"

The mist disappears, and I feel as if my feet land with a thud on the floor, the dreamlike haze vanishing. My hand drops from the door, and I turn around to see Nero standing there with a concerned gaze.

He eyes me up and down. "What are you doing?"

What am I doing? I look around and realize I'm in a place in the house I've never been in before.

"I... I don't know."

His forehead creases, and he steps forward, resting his hand on my shoulder. "What were you doing trying to get in that door?" He nods behind me, the coolness of his tone taking me back.

I turn and look at the door again, shaking my head. "I don't know."

He gently turns me back to face him. "C'mon. I'll take you back to your room."

I get the sense that he doesn't want me around this door, so I go with him.

"How did you know where I was?" I ask as we make our way down the gloomy hallway.

When he doesn't immediately answer, I look at him.

"I was watching you sleep, and I got hungry, so I went to the kitchen to grab something. When I came back, you were gone, so I went searching for you."

A normal person would be freaked out that he likes to watch me sleep. It's weird that I don't mind.

"I woke up, or I thought I did anyway. It was like a dream, but not. And this woman kept calling my name."

"Do you have a history of sleepwalking?" he asks.

I shake my head. "No. Never. It's weird, it felt like I was being led to that door."

He clears his throat and circles his head as though he's trying to work out a kink.

I stop and tug on his shirt. "Nero, where does that door lead?"

His gaze flicks over my face, and he holds the same look he does when he's hiding something. The same facial expression from that night at the motel parking lot. He's keeping things from me.

I wonder if it has something to do with the once-a-month Saturday nights. I'm pretty sure it does for no other reason than my gut is telling me it does. I think back to Anabelle and Rapsody telling me to ask Nero about it. He's been upfront now about his stalking regret and his childhood trauma, so how bad could those Saturday nights be that he's keeping it from me?

"Does it have something to do with all those expensive vehicles driving through Magnolia Bend on their way here once a month?"

His nostrils flare. "Let's get back to your room. We'll discuss it there."

My stomach bottoms out. So it does. And it's obvious from his reaction that he's not looking forward to telling me whatever it is.

I nod, and we walk through the communal part of the house, past the stained-glass raven, and to my bedroom.

Once we're inside, and he shuts the door, I whirl around. "Tell me. Whatever it is, just tell me."

He pushes his hands into his jeans pockets and stares at me, scanning me as if he's trying to memorize me. Does he think whatever he's going to tell me will change things for me? "That door leads to the basement of the manor."

I step closer to him. "What's in the basement, Nero?" I whisper as if I'm saying I can keep his secret.

"The Ritual Room."

I frown, not understanding. "What's the Ritual Room?"

He clears his throat and slides his hands out of his pockets, pushing one through his hair. "It's a sex club that my brothers and I run."

I blink and blink again. Out of all possible things, the rumors I've heard from bar patrons, that was not the answer I expected to hear. "A sex club?"

He nods. "You cannot tell anyone." His voice is serious, and if I'm honest, there's a bit of a threat in his tone.

"Of course not."

"I'm serious, Cinder. I'm not worried about myself, but powerful people attend every month, and if they found out that an outsider knew about it, they wouldn't hesitate to do what they had to in order to make the problem go away." His blue eyes burn into mine, and I realize that the threat in his voice is about my safety.

I rest my hand on his chest. "I understand."

He nods. "My father started it a long time ago, and when he died, Asher took over. As we all came of age, we joined."

"What happens down there? Is it just a big orgy once a month?"

He smirks. "Sometimes. There's a theme every month. People do whatever they want down there. That's the whole point."

My hand drops from his chest. "And you... you partake in all of this?" The image of him with another woman slams into

195

my mind, and I feel sick inside knowing on that Saturday, he had been with someone else.

"Usually." He shrugs. "Not lately, though."

My head tilts. "Why not?"

"Because there's only one woman these days that I have any interest in being with."

My shoulders sag in relief. There's one thing I need clarity about, though. "Why did you seem so nervous to tell me about it? I mean... I'm a stripper. I'm not exactly a saint."

"It's one of our family's most closely guarded secrets for one, and if it were to get out, it wouldn't affect just me, but my brothers as well. But mostly because I recently told you all this heinous shit from my past. I was afraid that if I piled on one more thing, maybe it would be too much, and you'd want to bail on us."

I place my palm on his cheek. "You worry too much."

His head slides along my palm, and he kisses it. "No, just a lot of experience with loss."

My heart stutters inside, and I wrap my arms around him. When he embraces me back, my body fills with a warm glow.

With my cheek pressed against his chest, I say, "Am I allowed to have fun with you in the Ritual Room?"

He unwraps his arms from around me and pushes me back by the shoulders. "You'd want that?"

I nod.

"The idea of performing sexual acts in front of other people doesn't freak you out?"

My head tilts. "I've been stripping for years. I've done VIP parties. It's nothing I'm not used to, only this would be different because... well, it's with you."

His gaze skirts around my face, as if he's really trying to see how comfortable I am with it. "If you seriously want that, there's more you should know."

My breath catches in my throat. I get the feeling that this is the part he was most nervous to tell me. "Okay..." Is he going to finally tell me he was engaged? Oh shit, he didn't take Maude down there, did he?

"I like to share my partners." He stills, bringing his thumb to his mouth, waiting for my reaction.

"You want me to have sex with another man? A woman?"

He nods.

God, why does the idea of performing with someone else for his pleasure turn me on so much? I love performing for him. When he's at T&T's, I get off seeing his shadow in that booth. What would it be like to have him watch me have sex with someone?

"I can be perfectly satisfied keeping things how they are." He squeezes my shoulders, his eyes imploring. "If it's not something you're into, that's fine. It's not something we have to explore."

His eyes look genuine, which makes me want to say yes even more than I already do.

"Nero, that's something that I'd like to try."

His eyes light up like the sky on a beautiful summer day. "Really?" I nod, and he palms the back of my head, dragging me in for a kiss. Before our kiss progresses to something more, he pulls away and rests his forehead on mine. "There's one more thing."

I lean back to meet his gaze. "What more could there be?"

"Everyone wears masks. There's a whole system I'll explain later, but what you need to know about is the initiation."

I swallow. "Tell me."

"Everyone has to do it. There are no exceptions."

"Nero, just tell me." My voice grows firmer.

"You'll have to be unmasked, and you'll have to do whatever I tell you in front of everyone. The whole thing will be recorded to use as leverage if you ever tried to use your knowledge of the club for your own gain or told anyone about it. It's why my dad started the club in the first place —so he'd have something to lord over all the other one-percenters. That, and intel. There's a lot that goes down in that club besides just sex. People talk, divulge things they shouldn't."

My hand goes to my stomach. "Okay, I can do that."

He cups my face and lowers himself so our eyes are level with each other. "Are you sure?"

"I am. Nero, I *want* to do this."

"Okay, then. Next Saturday, you'll be initiated in the Ritual Room." His lids grow heavy, and I know he's thinking about what might happen down there, as am I.

I press my thighs together, then a thought suddenly occurs to me. "Will Anabelle and Rapsody be down there?"

He nods. "Yeah. Asher and Anabelle keep things pretty private, but Kol and Rapsody have been known to put on a show. Though he'd rip off anyone's hand who tried to touch her."

"Will that be weird?" For the first time since this conversation started, I feel unsure of my decision.

He shrugs. "Only if we make it weird. Is it weird when you're naked in front of Lisa at T&T's?"

Good point. I shake my head.

"There you go. Speaking of..."

"What?"

He drops his hands from my face and steps back. "There's something I've been wanting to talk to you about, but I didn't know how to bring it up. Since we're laying it all out tonight, maybe this is a good time."

I nod for him to go on.

"I don't want you to work there anymore. I can't be there to watch you twenty-four-seven, even though you know I'd like to be." When I open my mouth to protest, he plows right on. "What if Freddie shows up there? He might be there for Lisa, but he saw you at the motel and might take it out on you."

"Nero, there's security there. I'll be fine."

He shakes his head. "Security might help if it's one-on-one. What if he shows up with a gun?"

I hadn't thought of that. Lisa says Freddie hasn't tried to contact her since everything went down that night, and she moved to the other hotel, but that doesn't mean he won't.

"It has nothing to do with controlling you, I swear. It's just about keeping you safe. Plus, you're with me now. You can do whatever you want with your life now that you're out from under your stepmother's thumb."

"Am I?" When Nero frowns and his forehead wrinkles, I add, "With you?"

"Haven't I made that obvious?" He places his hands on my hips, squeezing. "I thought it was clear that I'm completely obsessed with you."

I can't help but smile. "You have, but we haven't really discussed what that means. Are you my... boyfriend?"

He chuckles and gives me a chaste kiss. "Sure, I'm your boyfriend."

"Why are you laughing?" I lightly smack his shoulder.

"It just sounds trite compared to what I feel, but you can call me whatever you want, Cinder. I'm just going to call you mine."

My heart inflates so fast I fear it might explode. "I don't think you're trying to control me. You're justified in your thinking."

"But..."

"But I need to think about it."

He shakes his head and laughs. "You don't have to think

200

about wanting to join a sex club so I can share you, but you do have to think about whether or not you'll quit T&T's?"

I shrug. "I have to figure out what I want to do. So much has changed so fast for me."

He nods slowly. "Okay, I can understand that. Do you have any ideas?"

I think back to that motel room when I was teaching Dahlia to dance, and something lights up in my chest. "I do, but I want to make sure I'm heading down the right path. Just give me a bit."

He smiles. "I can do that."

Nero kisses me, which leads to him undressing me, which leads to so much more before a very sound sleep.

CHAPTER
TWENTY-TWO

NERO

The next morning, I text my brothers in our group chat and ask them to meet me in Asher's office that afternoon. I need to tell them that I'll be initiating Cinder into the Ritual Room.

When I walk in, they're already gathered, probably talking shit about me or talking about how they can "protect" me from myself. I steel myself against irritation, just wanting this to go well.

"What's with the summons, kid?" Kol asks as soon as I enter the room.

I glance around. Anabelle isn't here, which means Asher must've told her to leave us alone since those two are attached at the hip these days.

"It's not a summons. I just need to fill you in on something." I sit in the chair across from Sid.

His dark eyes narrow on me, a predator assessing. "He's bringing Cinder into the Ritual Room."

Fucking Sid.

Asher arches an eyebrow. "Is that true?"

I'd like to deny it just to prove Sid wrong, but I can't. "Yes. She'll go through initiation the next meeting."

They all look at one another. Asher at Kol. Kol at Sid. Sid at Asher. Each of them share the same question in their head.

"What?" I snipe.

"You know what it means to bring her in," Asher says in a grave voice.

I do. Cinder's not like everyone else there. She doesn't have a fortune and prestige to lose. Embarrassment if her tape ever got out, sure. But that pales in comparison to everyone else. If I bring her in, it means that she means something to me. Something more than just a fling, not just some girl I'm fucking. The same as when Asher brought Anabelle and Kol brought Rapsody. Sid will probably never bring a woman.

We fuck women in the Ritual Room, sure. And we fuck women out of it, but we never bring those women there. Not until Anabelle and Rapsody, anyway. So by bringing Cinder in, it means I plan to keep her around for the future.

Hell, I never even brought Maude. The idea of even telling her about the sex club was a non-starter. She never would've been into it and would have judged me for it.

But not Cinder. She's never judged me. She's perfect.

"I know what it means. And it's not a problem." I look each of them in the eye so they know I'm serious.

"Is your stalking still a problem?" Sid asks. "Is she going to freak out about it when your behavior escalates, and she finds out? Will she go off running for the hills, babbling all our secrets to anyone who will listen?"

"I told her. She knows I was watching her, and she knows what happened with Farrah in high school."

Sid's eyebrows hit his hairline in surprise. Finally, I shock the fucker.

"She was cool with it?" Kol asks.

"Yes, and she didn't balk when I told her about it or the Ritual Room."

Sid scoffs. "Probably because she's a fucking stripper. Probably seen more dicks in the VIP room for money than a proctologist."

I jump over the table, fisting the front of his shirt. "Don't you fucking dare talk about her like that."

Sid's face transforms from smooth and smug to rage. He pushes at my shoulders and stands, making me stumble back. "You'd better watch yourself, kid. Don't touch me ever."

"Enough!" Asher shouts.

My hands drop from Sid's shirt, eyes narrowed. "You of all people shouldn't be judging anyone. We all know you're fucked in the head."

Sid's hands clench at his sides, and he steps so our chests are brushing, but Kol puts his hands on each of our chests, pushing us back.

"Go walk it off, Sid. Let us deal with this." Kol pats his chest, and Sid meets his gaze then nods.

Those two have always been thick as thieves.

Sid steps back, and the blank expression, the one that gives away nothing, is back on his face as he fixes his cufflinks. "Consider that your one freebie. You lay hands on me again and you'll regret it." He leaves the room.

Asher pinches the bridge of his nose. "You know, I really thought that as I got older, I wouldn't have to referee fights between my younger brothers."

I motion in the direction Sid just left. "He shouldn't have said that shit about Cinder."

Asher looks at me and nods. Surprisingly, Kol does too, returning to his seat.

"You're right. If anyone had said anything like that about Anabelle, they'd probably find themselves in an unmarked grave in the family plot. I'm sure Kol agrees."

"Damn straight," Kol growls.

"But he has a point, Nero. Are you sure Cinder feels the same as you and is in this for the long haul? I'm not trying to sound like an asshole—"

"But he will." Kol laughs.

Asher gives him a scathing look. "But you were sure before with Maude and look how that turned out."

His words play at my biggest insecurity—that I'll be set as the fool again. Believe that someone actually cares for me only for it to be a lie.

"Cinder isn't Maude. I wouldn't have told her about everything if I thought she was. Not even Maude knew about the Ritual Room."

Asher nods. "Just make sure we don't regret it."

I feel as though someone just took a load of bricks off my chest. "No regrets. I promise."

I leave his office feeling good. Feeling lighter and better than I have... ever.

THE THEME for the Ritual Room tonight is medieval fantasy, and I picked Cinder's outfit knowing it would emphasize her tits, but I hadn't prepared myself for how fucking stunning she'd be.

She steps out of the bathroom wearing a barmaid outfit with a long brown skirt, a corset around her middle that cinches her waist, and plain cream cotton covering her swelling breasts. The moment I see her, I want to tug down the fabric and tongue her nipples, but it will have to wait. We're due in the basement for her initiation.

"You look absolutely stunning." I palm the back of her head, bringing her in for a kiss, but before it can lead anywhere, I pull away.

"I like this look on you." Cinder runs her hands up and down over my black velvet jacket with a half cape. She fingers one of the many buttons down the front, so I pull her hand away because it feels as though she's tugging on my dick, and if I don't stop her, we'll never make it out of this room.

"Are you ready for this?"

She nods, but I don't miss the way she chews on her lip. She's nervous, whether she'll admit it or not.

"Remember, you don't have to do anything you're not comfortable with. If you want to stop at any time, you tell me, okay?"

"Okay."

"Time for the final touch for my costume then." I step over to the table where I left my mask and slide it on.

"The raven. I guess I should have known." She runs her fingers over the long beak of my gold mask.

"And here is yours. You won't wear yours until next time, but I wanted you to see it." I hold it out to her.

It's much smaller than mine, but it's also gold. And because I want hers to echo my own, it has small feathers and a very small beak.

"I love it. Should I leave it here for tonight?"

I nod. "You won't be needing it. We should go though. Everyone will be waiting for us." I lead her by her hand down the dim hallway.

"I'm afraid I won't do well tonight. I want to please you," she says.

I tug on her hand and bring her to a stop. "That's something you don't have to worry about. You always please me. You just be yourself, okay?"

A long stream of air leaves her mouth. "Okay. Is there anything I should know before we go down there?"

We walk again.

"Just that I've already selected the people who will be helping with your initiation this evening." I squeeze her hand in reassurance. "And I suppose I should explain the mask system to you before we arrive. It won't matter much this time around, but in the months to come, it will."

"Okay..."

"You'll see that there're three different colored masks down there, beyond the gold ones my brothers and I wear, along with you, Anabelle, and Rapsody. Each color mask denotes something different. White is a watcher—pretty self-explanatory. They just want to observe and might choose to satisfy themselves. You won't see a lot of those. Red is a waiter—those people haven't decided what they're in the mood for. They can be approached and offered any number of things, then they'll decide what they're up for. There're lots of those. And then black. Black is a doer."

"What's a doer?"

"Those people are up for whatever. It implies that they've given their consent for any and everything. Part of what gets them off is not knowing what might come next. The rest of the guests can do whatever they want with them."

Her eyes widen. "Are there lots of those?"

I chuckle. "More than you'd think."

By the time I'm done explaining it, we've arrived at the basement door. The same one I found her sleepwalking to.

I pull the skeleton key from my pocket and insert it into the lock. "Last chance to back out."

Cinder's hand runs down my back to my ass, which she squeezes. "Not a chance."

My dick twitches in my pants. God, this woman.

I turn the key and swing open the door. It's time. Finally.

CHAPTER
TWENTY-THREE

CINDER

The large wooden door swings open to reveal a set of stairs carved out of stone and leading into darkness. Old sconces flicker on the wall, casting shadows.

I swallow. I wasn't lying when I told Nero that I have no reservations, but looking down into the blanket of darkness, my stomach turns over. Not because I'm unsure, but because I want this to go well. When we leave here tonight, I want him to have no doubt that I'm the right choice.

He takes my hand, and we slowly make our way down the steps. The number of stairs make it feel as if we're descending into the bowels of the earth. When we're at the bottom, we find ourselves at the end of a long hallway with doors on each side. Sensual music plays, thrumming through my body as we make our way down the hall.

"My brothers and I each have our own private rooms, and the others you can think of as theme rooms," Nero says.

As we approach the end of the hallway, murmurings can be heard over the music. Nero grips my hand tighter as though he can feel my anticipation growing and wants to ease my worry. I've performed enough that I'm not nervous to be in front of everyone in that sense—I don't have stage fright. But I feel like the first time I stepped on stage. I know what to expect now and the jitters have vanished, but tonight I'm on edge only from not knowing how it all goes down.

When we reach the end of the hallway, we enter a cavernous room filled with people wearing masks. As Nero said, they're all different colors, and everyone is also dressed in theme for tonight's event.

The crowd parts as if we're someone of importance. Never in my life have I felt that way. We make our way through them, and when we reach the other side, I see a dais. It's empty except for a large black chair with intricate gold detailing making it look like a throne in the center.

Nero holds my hand as he helps me up the stairs onto the dais and follows. Reaching for my hips, he turns me so I face the crowd as he stands behind me. I take in all the faces, the familiar lust filling their eyes through their masks and their slackened jaws from when I perform at T&T's. As it always does, a surge of confidence and power fills me.

Without saying a word to me, Nero palms my breasts, running his thumb over the thin cotton over my nipples. My eyes drift closed as my nipples peak. I'm panting, and when he cups the weight of my heavy breasts in his hands, a small moan slips from my lips.

He continues to fondle me, playing, tweaking, brushing my nipples just enough to drive me crazy and make me want more, until another man steps on stage with us. The man in a black mask comes to stand in front of me, and his hazel eyes roam over my body from top to bottom and back again.

"Oh, she's a sweet little thing, Nero. You were right," he says.

One of Nero's hands moves up from my breasts to wrap around my neck, and he speaks directly into my ear. "Carlos is going to suck your tits while I get you off with my fingers. It's a little warm-up for what's to come. Would you like that?"

I nod enthusiastically, my breath coming in raspy waves.

Carlos smiles, one corner of his lips lifting more than the other.

"Pull up her dress for me, Carlos," Nero says.

Carlos bends down and does what he says, pulling my skirt to my waist. I'm not wearing any underwear, and Nero's fingers immediately slip between my legs, finding my swollen clit. My ass arches out to grind against Nero's hard length between us.

Nero continues his ministrations while Carlos tugs down the elastic at the top of my shirt so that my breasts are bared for the crowd.

"Fuck, what gorgeous tits." Carlos palms them and tweaks my nipples.

My breath comes faster when he wraps his mouth around my nipple, sucking softly before the suction grows harder. Nero continues to own my pussy with his fingers, dipping them lower and collecting my arousal before bringing them back to my clit.

Carlos tugs on my nipple with his teeth, and all three of us watch as he pulls away from me. Eventually his mouth pops off my breast, and it jiggles.

Nero groans behind me and thrusts his hips into me to feel how much this is turning him on. That matched with his fingers and Carlos concentrating on my other breast is taking me to the edge fast. No way I'm going to last long.

Both men continue to torment me in the best way, then Nero says, "Let's switch."

Carlos grins at me again as Nero's fingers run along my lips, sliding into my mouth to lick off my arousal. Nero now plays with my tits and watches as Carlos's hand moves between my thighs. Nero keeps thrusting into my lower back, and it makes me want to be full of him. But I'm also enjoying the way Carlos has stripped his gaze off my face as he works between my legs.

Then Carlos's and my gazes lock and hold as he increases the pressure, and my core tightens.

Nero must sense me pulling back because he whispers, "Let go, princess. Let him see how beautiful you look when you come and know how lucky I am that you're mine."

His words send me over the edge, and I buck against Carlos's hand, my head falling against Nero's chest, crying out. Nero pinches my nipples—hard. My orgasm is heightened by all the eyes watching us.

When I finally come down, Nero uses his hand on my chin to turn my face, kissing me deeply. "Princess," he practically growls.

Somehow, I'm still able to stand, though my legs feel like jelly. With his hands around my waist, Nero turns me to face him, taking my hand and walking backward.

"Undo my pants and pull my dick out." The authoritative voice he commands me with is such a turn-on.

I reach down and undo his pants, slide the zipper down, and pull out his long length.

He runs the pad of his finger from my temple down to my chin then over my mouth. "We're going to put these plump lips to work. What do you think?"

I'm only able to nod.

Nero grips the base of his cock, tugging on himself. I can't help but watch. "Take all your clothes off. I want everyone who's not on this stage to know what they're missing out on."

My hands rise to unlace the corset around my waist, and I drop it to the floor, then I pull off my shirt. Finally, I yank the skirt down.

"Leave the shoes on," Nero says.

I might start leaving my shoes on even when we're not in the Ritual Room.

Nero steps back and sits on the throne. He looks like a king —legs splayed wide, stroking his thick, hard cock, the raven mask hiding his face except for his eyes that are eating me up and the insolent tilt to his chin that lets everyone know he's the one in charge tonight.

Nero slides his hand into the hair at the back of my head, pulling me toward his lap. "While you're working me, Carlos is going to make you come with his tongue. Let's show him how good you taste, shall we, princess?" I nod, and Nero urges my lips to the head of his cock. "Are you ready to show everyone why you're my queen?"

Jesus, I could melt into a puddle right here. This man and his words.

Without waiting for me to answer, he brings my mouth down onto him, and I open wide, taking in the length of him. He groans deep in his throat as Carlos's hands wrap around my waist. He tugs me back so my torso is parallel with the floor. With a hand on each ass cheek, Carlos spreads me.

The first flick of his tongue lands on my puckered hole, and I jolt, but I ease from the pleasure, moaning around Nero's cock. I work my lips up and down him, my gaze flicking up to his. He's torn between watching his dick disappear into my mouth and watching what Carlos is doing to me.

Because I can't fit him all in my mouth, I bring one hand to the base of his shaft, squeezing gently while I suck in my cheeks and run my mouth up and down his length.

Carlos shifts his attention to my opening, fucking me with his tongue. My eyes drift closed, and I moan. Nero's hand threads through the hair at the top of my head.

When I open my eyes, Nero and Carlos must share a look because Nero grins before his eyes fall down to mine and his dick twitches in my mouth. I swirl my tongue around his tip, then suck, fisting up and down his cock while Carlos moves onto my clit. His tongue flicks, then he sucks my greedy nub. With a few more of those moves, I'll be coming on his face in no time.

I'd forgotten about the crowd, but when I hear someone behind us moan, the people come to the front of mind again, and it only serves to ratchet up my desire.

"Make her come, Carlos." Nero smirks at me.

Carlos doubles his efforts, sucking and flicking and shoving his face between my legs. Like a large gust of wind, my orgasm blows over me, surrounding me and sending me flailing as I pop off of Nero's length and cry out, grinding against Carlos's face.

By the time my orgasm passes, and I stare up at Nero, his gaze is heavy-lidded.

"That will be all, Carlos," Nero says without his eyes straying from mine. He holds out a hand to help me to my feet, and I stand in front of him, my arousal dripping between my legs. "Now ride me. Take what you want... from me. Claim me as yours in front of all these people."

I waste no time straddling him, settling on his lap. There's room on the throne for my legs on either side of his, and I'm sure that's by design. Reaching down for his base, I slowly lower myself onto Nero. Our foreheads meet, and we groan in unison as my body grows used to the stretch of him. I move up and down, my body adjusting to his length.

"God, I love your fucking tits. They're so perfect, princess." He brings one to his mouth and sucks on my nipple.

My hand goes to the back of his head, holding him there, needing more.

There's something hot as hell about the fact that I'm naked, and he's completely clothed while I ride him. It makes me feel wanton, as if I'm at his mercy.

My movements are sharp as I slam down on him, unable to get enough—enough of this, of him, of *us*. My breasts rock each time, and the heavy weight of them bouncing sends sensation down to my clit.

Nero moves his hands to my waist, and I roll my hips against him, eager and desperate for the friction on my clit. The first flutters of my orgasm start in my womb. The sensation builds and builds, and though I try to clench it at bay, there's no way I can deny what my body demands.

I grip Nero's hair and cry out, pushing my tits into his face as I come hard. He bites one nipple, and it spurs another orgasm. He grips my hips hard, holding them in place and fucking me at a savage pace. His gaze fixates on my tits bouncing, and with one final thrust, he holds himself there, coming inside me. His cock jerks, then warmth spills out between my legs.

We remain in place, catching our breath, my face tucked into Nero's shoulder while he runs a hand up and down my back. A few seconds later, he taps my hip with his hand, and I pull back before he threads his hand through my hair and pulls me in for a savage kiss.

"You were perfect, just as I knew you would be," he says.

Physically, I expected to be satisfied tonight, but I couldn't have predicted how close I'd feel to Nero emotionally.

CHAPTER
TWENTY-FOUR

CINDER

I awaken late the next morning, and it takes me a moment to realize where I am.

Nero's room.

Last night after the Ritual Room, we came back here and showered—well, he showered me—then Nero applied lotion all over my body and combed my hair out before helping me into my pajamas and tucking me in.

I fell asleep with him wrapped around me and slept the most soundly I ever have.

I roll over to see Nero, but his side of the bed is empty. Frowning, I sit up. "Nero?"

He doesn't answer, which means he's not in the en suite or his walk-in closet. My shoulders deflate. I thought we were over the disappearing acts.

The bedroom door opens, and Nero steps in holding a tray filled with breakfast foods. He's shirtless, his defined muscles and large raven tattoo on display, with a pair of low-slung gray pajama pants on. Basically, he looks like a girl's wet dream.

"Good morning," he says. "Ready for breakfast in bed?"

I smile. "Only if you're joining me."

He steps to my side of the bed and places a chaste kiss on my mouth. "Try to stop me."

Nero sets the tray over my lap and rounds the bed to his side, crawling in.

The breakfast tray is filled with all my favorites, including the pastries I've gushed over since arriving at the manor.

"This is very sweet. Thank you." I give him a kiss.

"You deserve that and so much more," he says.

I chuckle. "Why? Because I performed so well last night?"

He shakes his head. "No, because you're you."

My stomach swoops. If I'm not careful, I'm going to completely fall for this man. If I could trust the universe to let me keep him, there would be nothing better. But what if it ends up like my parents, and the person I love most gets ripped away from me?

The closer Nero and I get, the more these kinds of doubts creep into my head even though I tell myself to enjoy the moment and stay in the present. But the fact that Nero still hasn't mentioned his engagement nags at me. Why is he still keeping things from me?

"Eat up," Nero says.

I fork a strawberry. "Have you already eaten?"

He nods. "I've been up for about an hour."

After placing my fork down and grabbing a pastry, I take a bite and moan. Nero's eyes grow heavy, and he watches my lips with intent.

A chuckle leaves my lips. "Sorry."

He leans against the headboard, fingers linked behind his head. "By all means, continue."

I laugh again. "I don't think I should. I have to get ready to go to work soon."

"At the bar?"

I nod with a mouth full of pastry.

"Have you given any more thought to what I said about quitting T&T's?" he asks.

I appreciate the space he's given me to try to sort myself out. "I have, but I don't know yet. It's taking me a bit to get my bearings. Going from having no options in my life to being able to decide for myself is a lot. But I promise I'm trying to come to a decision."

One thing that keeps coming to mind is how much I enjoyed teaching Dahlia to dance. But I'm not sure what that means quite yet.

Nero looks as though he wants to press the issue, but he presses his lips together and nods instead.

"You brought me enough food to feed an army. Are you sure you don't want any?" I change the topic of conversation.

He holds up a hand. "I'm good."

"Your loss," I say and pop a grape into my mouth.

"How are you feeling about last night now that you've slept on it?" he asks.

I tilt my head. "Why do I feel like I'm in a therapy session?"

He rolls his eyes. "I'm just checking in on you. Want to make sure you don't regret it."

When I finish chewing, I give him a chaste kiss. "Nero, I don't regret any of it."

A slow smile tilts his lips. "Glad to hear."

I think of how much my life has changed since this man brought me back here on New Year's Eve, and it almost seems unfathomable. "I don't think I have thanked you enough for letting me stay here. I hope you know how appreciative I am."

He coasts his knuckles down my cheeks. "No thanks needed."

"I don't know about that." I shake my head and grab a blueberry.

"Do you miss living in your family home?" His eyes fill with concern.

A frown tilts the corners of my lips. "I do. Though the more time that passes, the more I realize that maybe I was just trying to hold onto a time that was already lost. It's not like living there would bring my parents back, but I felt close to them there. Being away from it for a couple of months, I can see what a terrible situation I was in, and I know neither of my parents would've wanted that for me. I'll keep them in my heart and honor their memory without living in that house."

Nero takes my hand. "Good. I never want you to have regrets, especially when it comes to us."

LATE THAT NIGHT, I lock the door of Black Magic Bar and step out into the cool night air feeling less burdened than I can ever remember. I'm about to head to my car in the parking lot when something catches my eye.

There's a large FOR LEASE sign on one of the store fronts across the street. I'm pretty sure it's new, otherwise I would have noticed it before.

Hiking my purse up on my shoulder, I hustle across the road to take a look. I bring my face right up to the glass and put my hands on either side of my face to cut down on the reflection of the streetlight across the road.

The unit is a large open space and in need of some TLC. It was a thrift shop for a few years, but I don't know what it was before that. An idea takes shape in my mind—what if I could turn this place into a dance studio?

I know the answer as soon as the question hits my brain— yes.

It wouldn't be huge, just one studio, but that's all I would need.

Looking inside, I picture a small desk at the front when you walk in and mirrors on three of the walls, a ballet bar in front of each of them.

My stomach fizzes with excitement. I step back then fish my phone out of my purse to take a picture of the phone number to call. I tell myself not to get too excited as I shove my phone back in my purse and walk back across the street. Who knows what the rent is? Maybe they're asking for a crazy amount that I won't be able to afford. I have some money saved now that I no longer have to give Louise or Lisa a portion of what I make, but will it be enough?

And renovations to get the place in shape won't be cheap.

The buzz of excitement I felt fades as I unlock my car and slide inside. My shoulders sag, but I raise my chin before I pull out of the parking lot.

Whether I can afford this place or not, one good thing has come out of it—at least I now know exactly what I'd love to do with my life.

CHAPTER
TWENTY-FIVE

NERO

I go in search of Cinder, knowing where I'll find her.

When she returned from work last night, she didn't seek me out and went right to her room. I've resisted telling her I want her in my bed every night, not wanting to push her too much. So I forced myself not to look for her until after lunch and I had gotten some work done.

Music floats from behind the closed doors of the ballroom, and I smile, knowing she's inside. I slip inside quietly and arrange myself behind one of the large columns so I can watch her dance.

She's dressed in a black one-piece leotard with no sleeves as she bends and stretches to the music. The song she's dancing to has an upbeat tempo, and I assume she must have been here for a while already because there's a sheen to her skin and strands of hair have fallen out of her bun.

She is so fucking magnificent to watch. Whether I already had the proclivity or not, I could watch her all day. Her focus, the emotion that pours from her as she somehow interprets the words of the song and turns them into visual artistry.

The song ends, and she holds her pose before walking to her water and towel.

I clap, revealing myself, and walk out from behind the pillar. She whips around, startled, then smiles when she sees it's me. She bends down for her phone and turns off the music.

"How long were you watching?" Cinder tilts her head playfully before taking a long drink from her water.

God, it feels so good to have her know I like to watch and know she doesn't care or get weirded out.

"For most of that song, though I wish it were longer."

She chuckles and sets down the water, picking up her towel. "I like to dance when I have something I'm trying to sort out in my head. It's always helped me organize my thoughts, if only because I'm not focusing on it for a time. The problem always feels more surmountable after I dance." She pats the sweat from her face and neck with the towel.

I frown. "What problem are you dealing with?"

"More trying to figure out how to make something happen."

I study her for a beat, wanting to ask her, but Cinder usually isn't shy about telling me anything, and I told her the other day I'd give her more time to figure out what she wants. Even if it drives me crazy. "Are you done here for now?"

"Yeah, I'm tired."

"Why don't you get changed, then we can go for a walk around the manor grounds? I haven't even given you the full tour yet."

Her eyes light up. "That would be wonderful. I just need to have a quick shower first. Can you give me an hour?"

"Of course. I'll swing by your room to get you in an hour." I kiss her and wrap my arms around her body, loving the way she's still slicked with sweat because it reminds me of when we're having sex.

AN HOUR LATER, I lead Cinder onto the grounds of the manor.

"I love this time of year," she says, breathing deeply. "It always feels full of new possibilities. Plants start growing again and animals have their babies." She shrugs. "It just feels like a renewal of the earth. I like to think we're the same."

I link her fingers with mine, guiding her past the hedge maze.

"What's that?" she asks.

"A hedge maze. Fair warning, if you go in there, it could take you a while to get out. Though Anabelle's an expert now, so she could probably lead you through it quite easily."

"She is?"

I think back to Asher and Anabelle's journey to finding each other. "Long story." I squeeze her hand. "Now tell me what you have on your mind."

I should give her time, but I worry that her decision will take her away from me. I've stewed over it for the last hour, and I'm hoping she'll trust me to talk out what she's looking into. I'm thinking it has something to do with her looking inside the unit for lease close to Black Magic Bar.

"Well, I think I've figured out what I'd like to do if I left T&T's. I'm just trying to decide if I can make it work."

"What is it?"

I glance to my side, and she presses her lips together, almost as if she's nervous to tell me.

"I... I want to open a dance studio and teach kids." She whips her head to meet my gaze. "Sounds totally crazy and stupid, right?"

My forehead wrinkles. "Of course not. You're a wonderful dancer, and any child would be lucky to have you as their teacher. Is that why you were looking in that unit for rent last night?"

One corner of her lips lifts, but she doesn't mention how the only way I could know that is if I was watching her from afar.

"It is. I called the number first thing this morning, and I have enough money saved to afford the rent for a few months, but not enough to do the renovations that would be needed to convert it to a dance studio. I'm afraid that if I keep working and save enough money for the renos, the unit might be gone by then. But what choice do I have? I'll just have to keep saving and cross my fingers that it's still available when I am ready. Put my hands in destiny."

I pull her to a stop on the path. "What are you talking about? I'll pay for the renovations. Hell, I'll pay for the rent."

She shakes her head and drops my hand. "No. That's not why I'm telling you." She starts walking ahead on the path, and my steps grow faster to catch up.

"Cinder, I don't know if you know this, but I'm kind of a big deal."

She shakes her head but laughs.

"Seriously though, I have more money than I could ever spend in this lifetime. Let me pay for it all."

"But it means something to me."

I pull her to a stop, and she turns to face me, arms crossed, hip out.

"I want to see you live out your dream," I say in a low voice.

Her head tilts and her arms drop to her sides. "I want that too, but I can't take your money, Nero. It doesn't feel right. You've allowed me to live here without paying rent. You bought me all those clothes, and you feed me. You helped my friend. I cannot keep taking things from you. I'll figure it out, don't worry."

She turns to head down the path again, and I roll my eyes. "Why are you being so stubborn about this?"

"Because I don't want you thinking I'm only here for your money. It's the least interesting thing about you."

A warm sensation spreads through my chest. "Which is exactly why I want to help you."

She stops and spins to face me. "Nero, I can't take your money. But I appreciate the offer."

Jesus, why can't she see that it's not a big deal?

Time to change my angle. "What if it was a business loan? Would you let me loan you the money, and you can pay me back over time?"

She doesn't shoot me down right away, so hopefully I have her interested.

"How would that work?"

"I'd give you whatever money you need to get the place up and running, and every month you pay me a little back."

Her eyebrows raise to her hairline. "With interest."

I sigh. "Sure, with interest." Technically, if I charge her 0.25 percent, that would meet the terms of our agreement. "What do you say?"

She mulls it over. I see she still doesn't love the idea. I get she wants to do it on her own, but I want her to have her dream come true as fast as she does. Her happiness is my happiness.

"Okay, it's a deal."

"Great. And if you need any help on the business end, you can ask me." I pull her in for a kiss. "Now you can quit

T&T's, and I won't have to worry about that loose cannon showing up and hurting you."

"I don't think you have to worry about that anyway. Lisa said Freddie hasn't even tried to reach out to her since that night."

"Nonetheless, I'll feel better about it."

We walk again, and the horse stables come into view in the distance.

"What's that?" she asks.

"That's where we keep the horses."

Her eyes widen in excitement. "You have horses?"

"Would you like to meet them?"

"Absolutely!" Her pace increases.

If I'd known she was this into horses, I would've brought her out here a long time ago. I probably would have bought her a horse of her own.

We reach the stables.

"Wow, this is way nicer than the barn on my family property."

In truth, the horses here are probably living better than half the people in the country.

"You grew up with horses?" I place my hand on her lower back, guiding her to the first horse.

"We had two. They weren't anything fancy, but I used to love visiting them in the stables. Riding them, not so much. I never got very good at it. Do you ride?"

Nodding, I pet the horse. "I do. Though I haven't taken any of them out in a while."

"Who's this?" Cinder asks when she pets the caramel-colored horse.

"This is Umbra."

"Hi, Umbra." Cinder pets her, and it's easy to see that she's a natural. When her expression grows contemplative, I ask what she's thinking about. She sighs. "There's one thing I'm worried about, besides how much it's going to cost to do the renovations."

"What?" I rub a hand down her upper arm.

"Do you think that if people found out I used to be a stripper, they'd still bring their kids to be taught by me?"

I frown. "If they won't, then it's their loss. I've seen you dance, and I've seen you with Lisa's kids, and you're a natural at both. Don't let what other people think hold you back. People will come."

She twists her mouth. "I hope so." Then she drops her hand from Umbra and turns around to look at the other horses. Her eyes widen. "Oh my, who is this?"

Cinder beelines it to the other side of the aisle.

"That's Asher's horse, Poe. Be careful though, he's pretty temperamental. Just like his owner."

The shiny black stallion gives me a look as though he's not impressed by my words, but as soon as Cinder walks over to him, he turns his attention to her.

"Wow, he's huge!" She reaches to touch him, and I bolt forward, afraid Poe is going to freak out as he often does. But holy shit, he actually allows her to touch him.

When the horse leans down and rests his head on her shoulder, I openly gape. I push a hand through my hair. "Jesus, I've never seen Poe act like this with anyone. Even Asher."

Cinder smiles. "I've always felt a kinship with animals. There's this stray cat that hangs around the back of the bar, and I always sneak him food. He's so cute."

Watching her with Poe, I remember watching her with two terrified little girls and how she worked so well to calm them. For the first time ever, an inkling of wanting to be a father rushes through me. A part of me says to get her pregnant as fast as possible so that I can see her as a mother to our child.

I didn't even feel that way with Maude. Sure, I assumed we'd have kids one day, but it wasn't something I imagined or daydreamed about.

I come up behind her and kiss the back of her head, resting my hands through the belt loops of her jeans. "You're something else, you know that?"

She looks at me over her shoulder, beaming. "Because a temperamental horse likes me?"

"No, just because you're you."

When I tug her back into me by the belt loops, and she feels my hard length press against her, she lets out a soft moan. And when I yank her jeans down and make her come on my face a moment later in the stables, you'd better believe I give Poe a look of superiority. There's only room for one man in this woman's life, and I'm him.

CHAPTER
TWENTY-SIX

CINDER

Within a couple of weeks, I've quit my job at T&T's and signed the lease for the property on the main drag in Magnolia Bend. I was a little down the night I told Trina and everyone I wouldn't be returning, but as soon as I got the keys to the unit, my excitement kicked in.

I haven't decided what to name my studio yet, but that's okay because there's plenty to do to get the place ready.

Tonight, I'm meeting with the contractor I hired to do the work. When I leave my shift at Black Magic Bar, I walk across the street. I'm still working at the bar because I need to pay the rent on the studio until I have customers and bring some money in, but eventually I hope to leave that job behind as well.

I unlock the door, flick on the lights, and step inside. The place is a bit of a dump at the moment, but it's mine. I've never had a place, a thing, that was solely mine. I'm presently freeloading at Nero's place, and back when I lived with Louise, I begged for any small thing I got.

The sound of the door opening causes me to turn around. I smile when Jarvis, my contractor, walks inside. He's probably around Nero's age with sandy-colored hair and a matching beard. He's a good-looking guy, and if I wasn't already head over heels for someone, I might try to stoke the interest I've seen in the few times we've been together.

"Hey, Jarvis." I step forward and shake his hand. "Thanks for meeting me. I'm sure you'd rather be heading home at the end of the day than stopping here."

"On the contrary, I've been looking forward to this all day." He smiles, and I return it, though I drop his hand.

"Should we get started? I just want to go over some of the decisions I've made since we last spoke."

"Straight to business. Do you not like to have fun sometimes, Cinder?"

My mind immediately goes to the Ritual Room. "I have my moments, believe me."

He chuckles, then we discuss what I want done. I go through the list I have in my phone until we get to the last item. Last time we spoke, Jarvis pointed out that I could save some money if I didn't bring the mirrors all the way up to the ceiling, and since my clients are all going to be shorter than I am, I decided to take his advice.

"I think you're right about not bringing the mirrors all the way up to the ceiling."

He nods, hands on his hips. "All right, what were you thinking then?"

I glance around the space. "You didn't bring your ladder with you, did you?"

He shakes his head. "Sorry, left it at home."

Near the back of the unit, I spot one of those pails contractors use to mix paint or grout. That could work. I grab it and set it upside down on the floor.

"Not sure that's the most stable of things you want to be climbing on."

"Beggars can't be choosers. Can you give me your hand to help me balance?"

He holds out his hand, and I take it, gingerly climbing on the pail with one foot, then the second.

"Okay, I'm thinking to about here." I point at the wall.

With his free hand, Jarvis reaches into his pocket and pulls out a pencil for me. "Make a mark on the wall where you want it to end, then I'll measure it up."

I take the pencil from him and lean in, marking the wall. But my weight shifts, and the pail slides out from under my feet, sending me flailing toward the wall. Large hands grip my waist and prevent my head from crashing into the wall.

With all the adrenaline flowing through my veins, my heart beats a thousand times in the minute I take to compose myself. "That was close. Thank you."

"Told you," he says.

I turn around to roll my eyes at him but freeze seeing Nero near the front door. I didn't even hear him come in.

I'm never really sure when he's watching me. He doesn't tell me, and I recognize that the man has a life and a job that take up his time. But on the rare occasion I know he's there, I swear there's an inner glow inside me because I bask in his attention.

He's glaring at Jarvis as though he's deciding where to bury his body. I'm getting the strong message that even though Nero likes to share, he doesn't like another man's hands on me without his permission. I don't blame him. I'd be seething with jealousy if I saw another woman all over him.

I step away from Jarvis, and his hand drops from my waist. "Hey, I didn't know you were coming by." I walk over to Nero and place a kiss on his lips, lest there be any confusion where my affection lies.

"Thought I'd pop in and see how it's going."

We both know he was watching me from somewhere, but I don't say that. Instead, I take him by the hand and lead him over to Jarvis, trying to smooth this over.

"Nero, this is my contractor, Jarvis. He just saved me from smashing my head into the wall."

"Suppose I should thank him then." Nero's words are fine, but his tone and his clenched jaw make it clear he has no intention of thanking Jarvis for anything.

"Hey, man. Good to meet you." Jarvis sticks out his hand, but Nero just eyes it and doesn't move to reciprocate.

Nero turns to look at me. "You about done here?"

My cheeks heat with embarrassment at how awkward Nero is making this introduction. "Yeah, that was the last thing we had to go over."

"Great." He returns his attention to Jarvis. "You can see yourself out, right? You have a key?"

The way he's talking to Jarvis, the tone of his voice, it's how I would expect a billionaire to act and sound, but I've never seen that side of Nero.

Jarvis scratches the back of his head, clearly as uncomfortable as I am. "Yeah, of course."

"Great." Nero places his hand on my lower back. "Let's go."

I'm embarrassed and irritated, but I don't want to make Jarvis even more uncomfortable, so I just smile and nod and let Nero lead me out of the storefront.

Once we're on the sidewalk alone, I whirl around. "What was that?"

"What was what?" His tone is flippant once again.

"You were rude. Why?" My hands fall to my hips.

"You really have to ask?" He arches an eyebrow.

"Yeah, I do."

He shakes his head and walks toward the Black Magic Bar parking lot where my car is.

I stop at the edge of the parking lot. "Why are you walking away from me? We're having a conversation."

Nero spins toward me. "I walked in to the two of you giggling and another man's hands on you. What's to like about that?"

My arms flail at my sides. "You seemed to like it the last time it happened."

He narrows his eyes. "We both know that's different."

"How?"

"I'm the one calling the shots there. I decide what does and doesn't happen, and the other guy participating knows nothing is going to happen between you and him. It's purely sexual."

"Pretty sure Jarvis knows nothing is happening too."

Nero scoffs, and his head rolls back. "Are you kidding me? That guy wants to fuck you. It's all over his face."

I shrug. "So?"

His hands fist at his sides, and his jaw tics. "So?" He steps forward. "So... I don't like another man thinking he can try to steal what's mine."

"You're being ridiculous. No one is trying to steal anything, and if he ever did try something, I would put a stop to it. You embarrassed me in there. He's working for me, and you've made it super awkward."

He turns away from me and pushes a hand through his hair. "You don't get it."

"Nero, do you not think that some of the men I danced for at the club wanted to fuck me? You didn't seem to have any issue with that."

He grunts, keeping his back to me.

"I'm done with this conversation." I unlock my car and get into the driver's seat, slamming the door. When I put the key in the ignition and start the car, Nero turns around and faces me, so I roll the window down. "Let me know when you're ready to talk."

I reverse out of the spot and head back to Midnight Manor.

What the hell has gotten into him?

CHAPTER
TWENTY-SEVEN

NERO

My footfalls are heavy as I make my way to Cinder's room the next day.

I'd never seen her angry before last night, and I hate the way she left me standing in that parking lot. I wanted to run after her car and demand she stay by my side. But at the same time, it was clear she needed space from me. I just hope she'll feel like talking this morning.

When I reach the closed door of her bedroom, I hesitate before I knock. I hear shuffling behind the door, then it swings open.

"Hey." She looks at me briefly, then at the floor.

Fuck. My stomach bottoms out. She's clearly still pissed.

I clear my throat. "Can we talk?"

She doesn't say anything, but she does swing the door open wider and gestures for me to come in.

I turn to face her and push my hands into my pockets. "I want to apologize for my behavior last night."

She arches an eyebrow and crosses her arms. Clearly she's not going to make this easy on me.

"When I saw the two of you together, it didn't sit well because no one knows you're mine. We're pretty private about our relationship, which is fine, but... I don't know. Looking back on it, I think me being upset had more to do with watching you smile and laugh at him than it did with the fact that he wants you. That he touched you."

Her arms drop to her sides, and her shoulders sag, then she tilts her head. "You don't actually think I was entertaining the idea of starting something with him, do you?"

I shake my head and grip her shoulders. "No. I know you're not like that." I push at the voice in the back of my head that says I didn't think Maude was like that either. "You're not deceptive. I know that."

I tuck a loose strand of hair behind her ear, and her head tips back to look at me.

"I'm sorry I got heated last night," she says.

"You had every right to be. I was an asshole, and I'll apologize to Jarvis the next time I see him."

She places a palm on my cheek. "You don't have to do that. Just be nice the next time you come into the studio, and he's there, okay?"

"Okay." I place a quick kiss on her lips. "Does this mean we can get to the make-up sex now?"

She laughs and swats at me.

"I'm kidding. I have plans for us today. I know you're not working at the bar. Think you can drag yourself away from the studio for the day?"

Cinder trails a finger down my chest. "I think so. Jarvis is getting all the materials together so he can get started in there. There's not much I can do until his renovations are done besides deciding on a studio name and starting an online presence. But I think that can wait a day."

I grin, excited about what I have planned for us today. "Perfect."

"Are you going to tell me where we're going?"

I shake my head. "Not yet."

"But how will I know what to wear?" She bats her big blue eyes innocently as if they hold the power to break me.

"What you're wearing is fine. Now let's go." I take her hand and pull her toward the bedroom door.

"But I don't have my purse or anything."

"You don't need it."

We head through the manor, and I can feel the anticipation and excitement coming off of her. It's not until after we're in the car and we pull past the gates of the private airport that she tries to get me to divulge where we're going.

"We're flying wherever we're going?"

I glance at her. Her mouth hangs open at the private plane that waits for us on the runway.

"We are. Have you ever flown before?" I ask, parking the car.

"Once when I was a kid and my parents took me on vacation, but I barely remember it."

We both get out of the car and meet at the front, joining hands.

I squeeze hers. "Ready to join the mile high club?"

Her cheeks pinken. It's so fucking cute when she gets embarrassed. Given her sexual experience, you'd think it wouldn't happen so easily.

"How long is the flight?" she asks, ignoring my question.

I chuckle. "No way. If I tell you that, you'll have some idea of where we're going, and I want it to be a surprise."

She pouts, and it makes me want to bite her plump lip.

"You'll see soon enough." When we reach the stairs leading up into the plane, I motion for her to go first.

The entire plane ride, she watches out the window as though the landscape might give some clue as to where I'm taking her. I'm not worried—she's never going to guess.

The plane lands, and I escort her to the waiting vehicle that's taking us to our destination. Once we're in the back and the vehicle starts moving, Cinder shifts to look at me.

"Can I please have a clue?" She puts her hands in prayer pose in front of her.

I chuckle. "Were you like this as a kid before Christmas, wanting to know what presents you were going to get?"

She rolls her eyes. "Surprises make me itchy. I can't stop wondering."

I tap the end of her nose. "If you're patient, you'll find out in about twenty minutes."

"You're the worst." She slumps back in her seat like a sullen teenager.

I barely contain my laugh. I guess I know how to get under her skin now—act jealous and arrange a surprise for her, then refuse to say what it is.

"Are we going skydiving?"

I arch an eyebrow. "Wouldn't we have stayed at the airport?"

She twists her mouth. "Good point. Are we going to some fancy Michelin star restaurant?"

I glance at my casual clothes. "Dressed like this?"

She growls in frustration. "Right."

"Wait... would you go skydiving?"

She shrugs. "I don't know. Maybe if I didn't have time to think about it too much and freak myself out."

Noted for another time.

She taps her finger on her bottom lip, and I watch the movement the way a cheetah might watch a gazelle through the grass. "I know! Are we going to a sporting event?"

"That's a good guess, but no."

Her arms flail out in front of her. "That's it. I give up."

I grin. "Good, because we're here."

Cinder's head whips back toward the window as we pass the sign for the zoo. "We're going to the zoo?"

I shrug. "I know how much you love animals, so I got us a behind-the-scenes visit to the zoo. We'll be the only ones here today."

Her eyes widen. "In the whole zoo?"

I nod, amused by her reaction. "Yup. Just us."

"How did you do that?"

"With a very generous donation."

"Wow." She sits back, seeming to think for a moment. "Do you think we'll get to see any otters? They're so cute."

I wrap my hand around the back of her head and pull her face toward mine. "I think you can see whatever you want today. You say the word, and it's yours."

Her palm brushes down my cheek before she kisses me, showing me how grateful she is. "This is the best surprise ever, Nero. Thank you."

"Anything for you."

When the words leave my mouth, I realize how truthful they are. "Are you ready to show everyone why you're my queen?"

CHAPTER
TWENTY-EIGHT

NERO

The theme for tonight's Ritual Room is rock star, so I'm wearing leather pants with no shirt and a studded belt. Cinder just about blew me away when she arrived in my room wearing an early days Pamela-Anderson-inspired short black skirt with matching halter vest. Her cleavage is on full display, as are her shapely legs. She was made for the part.

"I like that you're not wearing a shirt." She traces her hand down my chest.

"You do, do you? What about you? You look like a wet dream tonight, princess." My dick twitches when I think of everyone looking at her and knowing she's mine.

I've already planned who will join us and our activities in my private room tonight, and I'm anxious to get there. But first, there's something else we have to do.

"May I put your mask on you for the first time?" I ask.

"Yes, of course." She's clearly excited by the prospect.

I walk to the table where she set it when she arrived and move behind her, I gently place it over her eyes and secure it in back.

When she turns around to face me, I can't help the word that slips out of my mouth. "Perfect."

She smiles when I slide on my own mask.

"Ready to do this?" I hold out my hand, and she accepts it.

"Yup. Though I'm wondering how things will go tonight now that I'm not being initiated."

We head out of my room into the hallway, where the sconces flicker on the wall.

"It'll start the same way most parties do. People will mingle, some will have a few drinks. From there, people will either wander off to the different rooms to start the fun, or they'll begin in the main room."

She licks her lips. "Is it weird that I feel more nervous about tonight than I did the night of initiation?"

My forehead wrinkles. "Why are you nervous about tonight?"

She shrugs. "I guess it's the idea of standing around and talking to all these people after what they saw last month."

I squeeze her hand as we enter the communal part of the manor. "Cinder, no one is judging you down there, believe me. They're all there for the same reason we are."

She nods, but my words haven't calmed her. I make a mental note to find Anabelle or Rapsody as soon as we get downstairs. She'll probably feel better around them.

When we reach the basement door, I take the key out of my pocket and unlock it to head downstairs. The bass of the music thrums as we make our way down the hall.

Unfortunately, it's not Anabelle or Rapsody I see when we enter the main room, but Sid. I haven't spoken to him since we got into it in Asher's office. Have barely seen him around for some reason. I'm not sure if that's by design or happenstance.

I'm still pissed off with him for what he said, but I'll try to keep the peace tonight if he's willing. You never know what mood he'll be in.

I nod as he approaches us, dark eyes taking us in through his wolf mask.

"Here to put on another show this month, Cinder?" he says.

So he isn't over our argument. I should be the one pissed off, not him.

Cinder doesn't say anything. Instead, she looks at me.

"Haven't seen you around the manor much. What have you been up to?" I ask, trying to get our conversation back on track.

Sid ignores me, sliding a hand around Cinder's waist and stepping into her. "C'mon, Cinder. You know how Nero likes to share."

Cinder draws back as much as she can, clearly uncomfortable with Sid.

I lean in so only the two of them can hear me. "Fuck off, Sid."

He turns his head in my direction. "Why should I? We've shared before. Many times. What makes her different?"

Everything I want to tell him, but now is not the time or place. We're supposed to be the leaders here, and everyone looks to us to set the standard.

"Save it for someplace else, and get your hands off of her."

He chuckles and releases her. "Haven't seen you like this since—"

"Enough!" I snap before he finishes the sentence.

He turns around and disappears into the crowd.

I set my hand on Cinder's lower back. "Sorry about that. He and I had it out last month, and he's clearly not over it. That was about the two of us, not you."

"Is he always so... antagonistic?"

I shake my head. "No, usually he's trying to make people think he's more civilized. That's what worries me."

Whatever. There's nothing to be done about it at the moment.

"C'mon. Let's go get a drink, and I'll introduce you to people."

An hour later, I catch Tristan's eye and nod toward my private room down the hall. He nods back.

I lean into Cinder and inhale her jasmine scent. "You ready for some fun?"

Her breath hitches, and she gives me a small nod. I look at Rapsody, who's she's chatting with.

"I'm going to steal her for the evening now. Have fun." I wink, and Rapsody blushes.

Taking Cinder's hand, I lead her down the hallway and unlock my personal room, bringing her inside. The room is dark and filled with the same music that plays in the main area. There's a bed against one wall and a dresser with various toys we could put into practice. There's also a bondage and milking table, which is where we're going to have our fun tonight.

As soon as we're in the room, I draw Cinder in for a kiss. I'm the only one who's ever going to kiss her from now on. I'm sure some guys would think it's messed up to want your woman to suck off someone else but not kiss them. For me, kissing is about intimacy whereas the rest is about physical pleasure. I don't want her sharing that intimacy with anyone but me.

She wraps her arms around my neck and returns the kiss. The leather of her top sticks to my bare chest while I palm the back of her head, pushing my fingers through her blonde hair. I sense the door of my room opening when the music gets louder for a moment, but I don't break the kiss.

Instead, I move my hands to her back and unzip her top, pulling away briefly to pull it up over her head, tossing it aside. When I move back in to continue our kiss, I slide down the zipper on her skirt, letting it drop to her feet.

The press of her hard nipples on my chest feels so good that I can't resist. I bend and suck one of her nipples, biting down on the tip and causing her hands to fly to the back of my head. Her fingernails run along my scalp as I devour her tit.

Tristan has been undressing behind her this whole time, watching us. He steps up behind her, whispering a kiss on her bare shoulder, and she startles, then meets my gaze and relaxes in my arms. His hand comes around, lifting her tit, offering it to me, and I wrap my lips around the nipple while his other hand delves between her legs. Cinder sighs when he touches her clit, her back falling to his chest.

I pull away from her breast and step back, wanting to admire them. I picture Tristan's cock nestled between her sculpted ass cheeks and watch as he pumps his hips into her.

"She's perfect, isn't she?" I say to him.

His eyes lift from kissing her neck, and he nods, running his fingers through her folds and squeezing her tit with his other hand. "These fucking tits, man." He kisses her neck, and she leans her head back, offering him more access.

"Make her come, and maybe I'll let you fuck them."

His grin says that's an easy task.

Tristan walks around her and settles on his knees in front of her. I watch as he dives right in between her legs, mouth feasting on her cunt, fingers between her legs. Cinder grips his head to keep her balance, breathing heavily and rocking her pussy against his mouth. It's hot as fuck that she maintains eye contact with me the whole time.

I undress while I watch them, first removing my boots, then my pants until I'm standing there naked, cock straining toward her as though it's a heat-seeking missile, and she is my target.

Her eyes flare once before she cries out and holds his head to her mound, riding out her orgasm. So. Fucking. Hot.

While she catches her breath, Tristan stands and looks at me. Cinder's arousal glistens on his face, and my hand reaches for my cock, stroking it.

"Now get on your knees for him, princess, and put him in your mouth."

She immediately does as I ask, and my cock jerks in my palm the moment she wraps her tiny hand around his girth and slides her lips over the crown. Cinder goes to town on him, and I know exactly what he's experiencing. Exactly how good she's making him feel.

"She's fucking magnificent at that, isn't she, Tristan?"

He tears his eyes from watching her and nods at me. "So bloody good."

I keep stroking my cock and walk around so that I can see her eyes. Tristan's hands are on the sides of her head as he rocks his hips into her mouth.

"You like him fucking your mouth, princess?" With my other hand, I squeeze my balls.

Cinder nods the little that she's able and gags when Tristan pushes even farther in.

"Fuck yeah, that's it," he groans, head tipped back.

Time to save him from himself. If he keeps going, he's going to be out of this.

"That's enough," I snap.

As I knew he would, Tristan lets go of her head and steps back. Cinder pulls away and looks to me for direction.

"Cinder, go lie face up on the black leather table over there." I motion in its direction and watch as Tristan tracks her every move with his gaze. "Tristan, grab the lube from the top drawer."

He does as I instruct and walks over to the side of the table.

"Spread it all over her tits. Don't miss any spots."

I walk to the head of the table and watch as Tristan squirts the lube all over her massive tits, then uses his hands to make sure it's been spread everywhere. Cinder's nipples are hard points, proof that she loves the attention. When he tugs on her nipples, she moans.

I lean forward and drag Cinder toward me so her head hangs off the table, then I look at Tristan. "Get up on the table, Tristan, and fuck her tits."

He wastes no time, hauling himself up and straddling her torso on the wide table. He pushes her tits together, sliding his cock between them until it disappears between the flesh. I imagine what that feels like, and from the expression on Tristan's face, it's pure ecstasy.

Unable to hold off any longer, I bring my dick to Cinder's mouth. She immediately opens for me. She moans as though it pleasures her to pleasure me, and my cock grows even harder. I hold either side of her head as I rock into her mouth. It's warm and wet and the way her throat squeezes around me when I push all the way in almost makes me forget my fucking name. Pure bliss. That's what this is.

Tristan meets my gaze, and we fuck her in different ways, one no less amazing than the other. When I think of the pleasure she's giving me, giving him, I almost bust a nut right then.

Cinder may dole out pleasure to other men when we're down here, but she's *mine*. Other men will only get a taste of the pleasure she can bring them. They'll never be able to keep her.

I can tell Tristan's close when his eyes drift closed, and he can no longer hold my gaze. With a couple more pumps and a groan, he releases ribbons of white that coat Cinder's chest.

"I wish you could see yourself, princess." I push in and out of her mouth as my balls tighten. "You look so beautiful."

When she moans, her throat squeezes the end of my cock, and I can't hold off any longer. I still, holding myself there for a moment, and decide at the last minute to pull out.

Jerking myself, I add my release to Tristan's, who's now climbed off the table.

"Fuck, that was incredible," I say.

Cinder's thighs are pressed together in need of her own release. Once I've ridden out my orgasm, I walk to the other end of the table, grab Cinder's ankles, and drag her down until her ass is near the edge. She meets my gaze, her eyes filled with need. My woman needs me to get her off, and I'll happily oblige. I grab her ankles again and position her legs so her feet are flat on the table, legs spread.

"Time for your reward." I grin and plant my face between

her legs until she screams, getting the same release she gave me.

CHAPTER
TWENTY-NINE

CINDER

I awaken in the same dream-like state I was in the night I found the door to the Ritual Room. Mist surrounds me once again, but I'm still in my bedroom. Pushing off the covers, I slide out of bed and walk toward the door, only I feel as if I'm floating instead of walking.

I don't have any control over my movements as I creep past the threshold. The mist overflows into the hallway, and I can just barely see the flickering of the wall sconces. Still, I push forward as though I know where I'm going, where I'm headed, but I don't.

The female voice from before urges me forward, calling my name.

I'm not sure how long I walk—it could be minutes, it could be hours—but eventually I find myself walking past the ballroom. I want to stop there. I like the ballroom. But I'm not allowed to.

Continuing down the hallway, the mist swirls at my feet. I find myself with my hand on the door to the aviary. Unlike the handle to the basement that night, this one is unlocked, and I push open the door, stepping inside.

Again, the mist clears as if someone snapped their fingers, and I'm back in control of my body again. I blink a few times when I see Nero sitting straight ahead with his back to me. He's leaning forward with his hands pushed into his hair.

"What are you doing here in the middle of the night?" I ask.

He startles, obviously not having heard me come in. "I could ask you the same thing."

There's pain in his eyes, though I can't fathom why. I move to him and crawl onto his lap, hugging him.

"What's wrong?" I ask in a soft voice.

He's quiet for a long moment. "There's something I have to tell you. Something I've been keeping from you."

I stiffen on his lap but force myself to relax. All his other omissions I was able to handle. Surely this one is no different. "What is it?"

He heaves out a long sigh. "I was engaged, and I called off the wedding right before I started coming in to watch you dance. Before my obsession with you."

Guilt weighs heavy in his eyes, and I don't know what to do with it.

Because I've been lying to him too.

"Okay..." is all I manage to say.

"I wanted to tell you sooner, but I was afraid you'd think you were a rebound or something, and you most definitely are not. I didn't expect to get this attached to you. I thought my obsession with you would fade with time, but it only grew."

I'd laugh at the irony if I didn't want to cry. "Are you telling me this because you still have feelings for her?"

His eyes widen. "No! God, no. She turned out to be a liar of the worst kind. But I didn't want you to think that I did if I told you too soon."

I brush my fingers through the hair at the side of his head. "It's not like I didn't think you had any relationships before me."

He shakes his head. "This is different. This was an engagement. We were months away from our wedding. I thought I was going to spend the rest of my life with Maude. Every time I tried to tell you, I'd balk. Then so much time had passed that I didn't know how to bring it up. It's just kept weighing on me more and more."

The mention of her name is like an ice pick to my chest, but I stifle my cringe. Should I tell him who Maude is to me? I'm afraid to for the same reasons he was afraid to tell me about their engagement.

I open my mouth to confess, but that's not what comes out. "I understand why you didn't say anything." I understand better than anyone. "But you should know that I don't doubt that whatever you feel for me is real and has nothing to do with your past."

"Really?" Hope springs in his eyes, dismantling the guilt.

I nod. "Really."

I kiss him. Nero runs his tongue along the seam of my lips, and I open for him. Our pace is slow and sensual as our hands explore each other's body. I push mine into his hair, and Nero rubs one hand over my breast, thumbing a nipple. It puckers, and he swallows my moan.

This man undoes me, and I did not see it coming.

Lips still on mine, Nero undresses me, slowly undoing the buttons on my pajama top and sliding the fabric off my shoulders. He kneads my naked breasts as I arch into his grip. My hands slide down to the hem of his T-shirt and pull it up and over his head, momentarily parting from our kiss. But as soon as the T-shirt is out of the way, he cups my chin and uses his leverage to direct my position in our kiss how he wants it.

He stands, lifting me with him in one swift motion, and I yelp, pulling away from our kiss.

"You're good, princess. I'll never let you fall." He meets my gaze as he slides my pajama bottoms over my hips, allowing them to fall to the floor. Then I do the same to him.

We stand completely bared to each other and somehow it feels soul deep, not just physical. But how could it be when I'm still keeping something from him?

With great effort, I push that thought from my mind. This is about the here and now.

Nero takes my hand and leads me to the large chaise. Because it's the middle of the night, the birds are quiet, and only the sounds of our breathing echo around us.

I lie down, and Nero moves over me, holding himself above me, but I wrap an arm around his neck and tug him down, wanting to feel his weight on me. Our mouths meet again, and we sink into the kiss, unhurried. His hard length sits snug between us, and I spread my legs so that he can tuck himself between my thighs. He pushes at my entrance, and I stretch around his girth, sighing into the kiss.

He gently rocks into me at a leisurely pace. Neither of us is chasing an orgasm. We're both content to enjoy each other's body and the connection we share.

Nero pulls away from our kiss, and I want to drag him back, but our eyes meet and hold, blue on blue. A vast well of emotion fills his. I don't need any more words of assurance from him. He feels the same way I do.

We continue to watch each other as he slides in and out of me.

"Touch yourself, princess." He leans down and kisses me before pulling away again.

I slide my hand between our bodies and sigh when I connect to my clit. I keep my efforts at the same pace as he's moving, and slowly, my orgasm builds.

My breathing picks up as we continue to watch each other. The swell of emotion between us grows larger and more intense, mimicking the pace of my impending orgasm.

When it finally hits me with full force, I stifle my cry, my back rising off the chaise.

Nero holds himself inside me and groans quietly into the curve of my neck as he rides out his own climax. Then he cups the sides of my face, and his gaze lands on mine, almost as though he's taking me in, capturing this moment to examine at some point in the future.

"That was..."

"Yeah," he says in a soft, gentle voice. "It was."

He bends and kisses me.

We stay wrapped in each other's arms, neither of us wanting to disentangle from the other. I fight to keep my eyes open, not wanting this moment to end.

As my body relaxes and my eyelids fall closed, he says, "I love you, Cinder."

Maybe it's a dream, because fate has always destroyed the people I love most.

CHAPTER
THIRTY

CINDER

The past couple of weeks with Nero have been magical. Ever since the night we spent in the aviary, something shifted between us, brought us closer emotionally.

No longer do I sleep in my own room. In fact, Nero had all my belongings moved into his room, so every night we fall asleep after sex in a sweaty, exhausted heap tangled around each other. It's everything I've ever wanted. He hasn't said the three words since, so I'm not sure if I dreamed them or not that night, but I've never felt so loved in my life, except by my parents.

Another thing that changed is that we eat our breakfast in the dining room with the other two couples and Sid. Though Kol and Rapsody are missing this morning.

"Where did you say Rapsody is?" I ask Anabelle seated beside me.

She passes me the plate with pastries on it, knowing by now that I add one to my plate every morning. "There's an art dealer in New York interested in some of her paintings, so they flew up there last night to meet with him today."

"That's so exciting. I hope everything goes well for her."

Rapsody brought me to the conservatory last week to show me some of her work. It's beautiful. Erotic as hell, but beautiful.

"Yeah, me too. I'm sure it will though. She's very talented."

"If it doesn't, I'm sure Kol will use his persuasive powers to make sure it goes how she wishes," Asher says wryly before taking a sip of his coffee.

I can see that. Kol is definitely protective of Rapsody. All the Voss men seem to be that way with their partners.

"What are you up to today?" Anabelle asks.

I finish chewing my bite of pastry. "Now that the construction is done, I'm heading into the studio to do some last-minute things before the official opening."

Lately, I haven't been able to stop smiling, and Anabelle's smile grows wider seeing mine.

"How's it going? Do you have anyone signed up yet?" Anabelle asks as she pours herself some coffee.

I smile at Nero on my other side. "I do because Nero surprised me and ran some ads in all the local papers and has an online campaign going on socials, which is funny since I don't even have my own personal profile on social media." I knock him with my shoulder. "There have been more inquiries than I thought I'd have at this point, which is amazing, but I still need to firm up my schedule. Figure out what classes I'll teach when and for what age group. It's going to take a bit of tinkering."

"You'll get it all sorted," Nero says and squeezes my knee under the table.

I glance at Sid, who sits alone on his side of the table since Rapsody and Kol aren't here. He's watching us intently, and I shift in my seat. I haven't asked Nero, but I don't think the two of them have cleared the air, since they never utter a word to each other. I don't know what went down between them. Nero just told me it was "brother stuff."

"I hope so. I just really want everything to go well. It's a lot of moving parts."

"Pretty sure all your parts were moving down at T&T's, weren't they?" Sid asks.

My face instantly heats, and my eyes fall to my half-eaten plate.

Nero flies up from his chair. "Apologize. Now."

Sid smirks. "Or what, kid? What are you going to do about it?"

"Enough!" Asher slams his fist down on the table, and I jolt. "I don't know what your problem is lately, Obsidian, but you've been a moody bastard for a while now. If you can't respect everyone who sits at this table, then I suggest you don't join us again until you can."

My eyes widen, and I glance at Asher. Anabelle's hand covers mine and squeezes.

"Happily," Sid says, tossing his napkin on the table and standing from his chair. He glares at all of us before he turns on his heel and leaves the room.

Nero sits back down and wraps his arm around my shoulders. "Are you okay?"

I give him a shaky nod.

"I'm sorry he spoke to you that way. He, of all people, should know better."

"Nero..." Asher says in what sounds like a warning.

I don't know what Nero means by his words, but I give him a small smile anyway, appreciating that he's trying to make me feel better.

"I think I'm full. I should probably get to the studio." I pick up the napkin off my lap and place it beside my plate.

"Let me walk you out," Nero says.

He accompanies me through the house, and when we get outside, I stop in my tracks. My shitty old car isn't there. In its place is a shiny new luxury car.

"Where's my car?" I ask Nero.

"It's right here." He gestures to the vehicle that I'm sure cost more than I've ever made in a year. Probably two.

"No, that is not my car."

"It is now. I couldn't stand the idea of you driving around in that unreliable one. It was a deathtrap."

I have no argument. That car was well past its prime. "It's

not like I drive that far. I literally just drive down the hill into town."

He comes around me and places his hands on my hips. "I need to know that you're safe."

I cradle his cheek with my palm. "That's very sweet. But this is way too expensive. I can't accept it."

"Can and will." He reaches into his pocket and pulls out a set of keys. "Here you go. There's no actual key to start the car, but you need them on you for the engine to start."

I sigh. "We're going to talk about this later, understand?"

"Sure. Totally understand."

I roll my eyes and shake my head, knowing I'll get nowhere with him. "Well, thank you very much." I give him a chaste kiss. "I'll be sure to show you how appreciative I am this evening."

He grins and slides his hands around me, squeezing my ass. "I look forward to it."

I laugh and swat them away. "Okay, I need to leave, otherwise I never will."

It takes me a moment once I'm in the car to make sense of the dash and where everything is. I've never driven anything like this. During the entire short drive to the studio, I'm paranoid that I'm going to crash the car, driving like a grandma, but my worries fade when I park in front of the studio.

I get out and stop on the sidewalk, admiring the sign I had installed above the storefront yesterday.

GLASS SLIPPER DANCE STUDIO

It took a while to figure out the name of the studio, but it felt right the minute the words glass slipper came to mind. It represents transformation, and if you're going to wear a glass slipper, you have to be light on your feet. You have to be intentional about where you place your weight on the bottom of your feet, and you have to move with confidence. All things that are important when you dance.

With a smile still on my face, I unlock the front door and step into what I hope is the start of a new beginning.

I've worked all day, cleaning up the construction mess and responding to parents' inquiries. My grand opening is next week, and I still have to figure out the schedule of classes, which is next on my list. After that, I need to tackle getting my account set up with one of the point-of-sale companies so that I can take payments in the studio.

I'm in the back storage room, looking for the paper I bought to fill the new printer, when the chime rings over the front door. I startle but relax, knowing it's probably Nero. Or maybe Anabelle came by to check things out. I told her she's welcome anytime.

I exit the storage room, and my smile slides off my face and down to the floor as though it's been melted off.

Louise and Maude narrow their eyes at me.

My heart hammers, and a whooshing sound fills my ears.

"Are you not going to say how good it is to see us?" Louise sneers. "After all, it's been quite a while."

"Wha... what are you doing here?"

Now that the initial shock has worn off, panic consumes me. Are they here to hurt me? Do they know about Nero and me? Have they talked to him?

In an instant, I worry they'll strip everything I care about away from me. Part of me always knew they would come back and ruin anything good I've made of myself. The universe has never been kind to me, not allowing me to keep the people I love most.

"We wanted to congratulate you on your big accomplishment," Louise says.

"Seems things have really turned around for you since you left home," Maude says.

"You should go." I step toward them to shoo them out.

"We're not going anywhere until you explain to me how it is that you hooked up with my ex-fiancé." Maude's face is red, her jaw clenched. I've never seen her this angry before.

My eyes widen. I don't know what to say. They obviously know, so there's no point denying it. The question is—what will they do with the information?

"What do you have to say for yourself?" Maude takes a threatening step toward me, and I freeze, unable to move my feet.

"Hey! What the hell is going on here?"

I squeeze my eyes shut at Nero's voice. Pain lances my chest because this is the beginning of the end of my happiness.

THIRTY-ONE

NERO

I blink, not sure I'm seeing what I am.

Cinder is with my ex-fiancée and her mother. And from the looks of what I just walked in on, they know each other. But how is that possible?

I came down to drag Cinder back to the house for the night. I'd planned to draw her a bath after dinner, knowing she's been stressed about the impending opening of the studio and has been putting in longer hours than Asher.

"Hey! What the hell is going on here?" I shout when Maude steps toward Cinder as though she's going to hurt her physically.

Cinder's eyes squeeze shut at the sound of my voice, and Maude and Louise turn around to face me. This is the first time I've set eyes on Maude since I broke up with her, and I'm relieved to find that there are no lingering feelings. In fact, seeing her and Cinder in the same room, knowing everything about the two of them, it makes me wonder how I could ever have fallen for Maude in the first place.

"How did you find me?" Cinder asks.

They both turn back in her direction. I walk around them and stand at Cinder's side.

"If you're trying to ghost someone, you should be careful about splashing your picture all over social media to promote your new business. It took hardly any digging to find out where you'd been living and who exactly you'd been spending time with." Louise looks at me with disgust and scoffs.

I look between them, confused.

"Was it her big tits, Nero? Is that how she seduced you away from me?" Maude asks.

"Cinder." I turn to face her. "How do you know them?"

Her blue gaze doesn't meet mine, and my stomach sours.

"I'm her stepmother," Louise says.

"And I'm her stepsister," Maude adds.

A single tear cascades down Cinder's cheek.

"Is that true?" I ask, feeling like my chest is caving in. It's hard to breathe.

She nods and opens her eyes, which are filled with guilt and sorrow.

I stumble back.

"That's right. You've been fucking your ex-fiancée's sister!" Maude shouts.

My mind races with thoughts. Piecing their relationship together, everything that Cinder told me about her childhood runs through my mind. These two people tormented a child and made her life a living hell. The anger over my own childhood rises, overtaking the fact that Cinder lied to me, too.

I whip my head toward Louise and Maude. "You. You're the one who treated a child with such cruelty after she lost her father." I step toward them. "You nearly starved her. Forced her to work at a strip club and give you her earnings." I get closer to them. "She's been working her ass off at two jobs while you two treat her like a servant. Actually, less than." My fists clutch at my sides.

Louise's head rears back, looking affronted by my accusations, but she doesn't deny them. "I always knew she was a vile little creature. And look what she's done with you. Seems I was proven right."

My nostrils flare, and I attempt to rein in my temper. "Have you forgotten that your daughter was fucking someone else behind my back while she was engaged to me?"

Maude has the good sense to look contrite. "I told you it was a mistake. I've missed you so much, Nero. What we had was so good." She walks right to me, way too close, and rests her palm on my chest, looking up at me and batting her eyelashes as if she's so innocent.

"What we had was a lie," I sneer. Then I look over my shoulder at Cinder. "Just like what we had. All fucking liars."

I can't deal with this anymore.

I turn back to Louise and Maude. "You two need to leave. You've accomplished what you set out to do. Now go." When they don't start toward the exit immediately, I shout, "Now!"

They flinch and look at one another before slithering to the door like the snakes they are. The two of them make me sick with how they treated a child deep in the throes of grief.

Steeling myself against what I feel for her, I turn back to Cinder. "I don't have anything to say to you either."

Her back hunches, and she breaks down in tears. I force myself to walk out the door, even though the urge to comfort her swells inside me like a tidal wave.

HALF A BOTTLE OF WHISKEY LATER, I'm still plagued by anger and pain, but the knife's edge has dulled, and it feels more tolerable at least.

I'm sitting on the same chaise in the aviary that Cinder and I made love on. At least, that's what I thought we were doing. Maybe that was all a lie too.

Attempting to put all my thoughts in order is proving more difficult due to the haze of the alcohol. I wonder again if it was indeed Asher who sent me that photo of Maude and the other guy. Cinder clearly hates her family, so she looks like suspect number one now. A great way to get back at her stepmother and stepsister. But that would mean she knew who I was before we started what we have. This entire time I've housed her, she was pretending to love me. Could I be that stupid, to be fooled by a woman twice in a year?

I set the bottle on the table beside the chaise just as the door behind me opens. I don't need to turn around to know who it is. I knew Cinder would come looking for me.

"What do you want?" I ask without turning around.

She steps into view. It's obvious from how red and swollen her eyes are that she's been crying since I left her hours ago.

Even the birds quiet down as if they're waiting for her excuses, too.

"I want to explain."

My eyes close for a moment because I hate hearing the pain in her voice. It makes me want to pull her into my lap and tell her that everything will be okay. But it won't be. She lied to me, and now I can't trust her.

"Sure, can't wait to hear this," I say.

She comes around to stand in front of me, and I motion for her to sit in the chair to the side of me, so I don't have to look at her head-on. I don't trust myself to be strong enough to push her away.

"Nero, you have to know that I wanted to tell you. I really did."

A caustic laugh leaves my lips. "Then why didn't you?"

"I was afraid of what you'd think."

"And what's that?" I turn to meet her gaze because I want to see for myself whether she's telling the truth or not. Of course, I couldn't tell that she's been lying to me this entire time so what do I know?

"That you would think my feelings for you weren't real." She holds my gaze until I'm the one who looks away.

I don't want to talk about feelings. I want answers.

"I blamed Asher for sending me the picture of Maude and another guy." I side-glance at her as her chin falls to her chest. "He denied it, but I figured he was lying."

Still she says nothing.

"After my anger wore off, I figured he did me a favor. And then I was drinking away the blues, so I wasn't thinking clearly, and I saw you for the first time. And you became all I could think about."

"Nero—"

I don't allow her to interrupt me, especially since my gut was correct. "You know I've been giving this some thought. I bet if I went back and did some digging, the picture came from you." I turn to look at her, arching an eyebrow.

She bursts into tears, burying her face in her hands. "Yes. I sent it." She cries for another minute and eventually pulls her shit together enough to wipe the tears from her face and look at me. "There's something you don't know."

"Oh, great. What?" I roll my eyes and blow out a breath of frustration.

"The night of the ball. I... was there."

My memories travel back to that night, but I don't remember seeing her. I for sure would have clicked with her. It was the night I proposed and had Asher... oh... fuck no. "We danced."

She nods.

"That guy was all over you, and I pretended to be..." It all comes back.

She nods, her eyes reminding me of that dance and how I couldn't get her out of my mind even though I was engaged to someone else.

"Maude didn't add you to the guest list."

"I snuck in. Louise ruined my dress that night and gave me a list of chores, but I hurried through them and altered my dress so I could attend."

"But..." Fuck, it was her. How did I never realize that or recall her?

"After that dance, I realized you were so nice and charming and such a good guy. I didn't want you to get mixed up with Maude. I couldn't stand the thought of you being fooled by her and tied to her for life. She's a horrible person, and she masked that from you. When I overheard her planning to meet up with another man, I had to do something to save you from the same fate I had. She and Louise talked about how she needed to make sure she got pregnant as soon as you guys were married to secure her position and your financial support for life. I couldn't let her trick you."

I won't tell her, but she did do me a favor. The idea of Maude being pregnant with my child and having to deal with her for the rest of my life sounds like a special sort of hell. But Cinder could have told me, instead of lying to me all this time. Why must everyone I care about lie to me?

"And then what?"

She wipes her cheeks. "What do you mean?"

I lean in closer to her. "What was the next part of your plan?"

She shakes her head. "I... I didn't have one. You guys broke up."

"You're lying, Cinder."

"I didn't have a plan after that. I just wanted you to know who she really was. But then you came into T&T's..."

I nod. "Continue."

Her eyes fill with a plea to forgive her. "You came into T&T's. I didn't even know who you were, but I was drawn to the stranger in the dark booth at the back. Then I went to the VIP room and..."

I motion with my hand for her to continue.

"When I saw you, I recognized you. I should have told you who I was then, but... I don't know... I hate my stepsister, and the idea of giving you a lap dance felt good. Felt like retribution in a weird way. I thought I'd give you a lap dance, and you'd leave. Your fascination with me would come to an end, you'd stop coming into T&T's. If I'd known... I mean... I had no way of knowing that—"

"I'd get you off?" I snipe, making it sound cheap and dirty when it felt anything but.

She nods. "I didn't expect that to happen. Then you brought me here, and it was only supposed to be for one night, but..." Her face twists.

I don't have time to respond before she spills her guts further. "But I got to know you, started to fall for you, fell... in love with you."

I slam down the whiskey bottle, and she winces, drawing back in the chair. "You don't get to whip those words out now!" A large lump forms in my throat. I thought that when we exchanged those words for the first time, it would be something special, not in the midst of our breakup.

Tears build in her eyes again. "I'm sorry, but they took so much away from me. I couldn't let them take you away too because of who Maude was to me. I wanted to tell you, I should have... I was just so scared. But I would have... eventually."

I squeeze my eyes shut, wanting so badly to believe her, but too many times I've given people the benefit of the doubt, and I'm the one who gets burned. "I don't believe you. You were never going to tell me. I'm convinced of that."

Her face crumples, and she reaches for me. I pull my hand away so she doesn't make contact.

"I swear to you I wanted so badly to tell you, but the more time that passed, the harder it got. Don't you understand? There's a reason you waited to tell me you were engaged."

I scowl at her. "My engagement had nothing to do with you. At all. And the fact is, I did tell you. But you being Maude's stepsister has everything to do with me. It's not the same thing."

She shakes her head. "Please don't let this ruin what we have. Please." Her voice is hoarse, holding a desperate plea.

"There's something I've been wondering. How come I never met or saw you when I was at the house?"

A flash of pain crosses her face. "They'd never let me come down from the attic whenever you were there. Louise would lock me in my room."

My fist tightens on my thigh. I shouldn't give a shit how they treated her, but it still pisses me off. I nod and stand from the chair, needing to get away from her.

"Wait!" Cinder rushes to her feet and grips my shirt. "Please don't leave like this. Tell me we can figure this out. I know you feel what I do, Nero."

I pull her hands off me, hating myself for having the urge to continue holding onto her. "What I *felt* for you, Cinder. Felt."

She shakes her head and tears burst from her eyes. "No. What we have is too good to be ruined because of them."

I frown. "It's over, but I'll admit, a part of me wishes you weren't so hard to walk away from."

She collapses to the floor in sobs as I turn and walk away from her. I have nothing more to say.

CHAPTER
THIRTY-TWO

CINDER

"Another one," I say.

I finished my shift at Black Magic Bar earlier this evening, and I've been drinking at the bar ever since. Two weeks have passed since my world fell apart. Nero still won't speak to me, and I've lost hope that he ever will again.

Anabelle saw me the night everything happened and was nice enough to insist that I stay in the west wing with her and Asher, so at least I'm not homeless. I ended up delaying the opening of the studio. I just couldn't find the energy to care to do everything that needed to be done. I've been so depressed I barely get out of bed in the mornings.

"Told you she'd be here."

When I hear Anabelle's voice, I turn around to see her and Rapsody standing a few feet back from the bar with concerned looks on their faces. They sit on either side of me.

"What are you guys doing here?" I ask. "Asher send you here to tell me that I'm no longer welcome at the manor?"

Anabelle frowns. "Never. I've made my position well known."

I squeeze her hand because that's really nice of her.

"How are you?" Rapsody asks.

I turn to her. "Lost. I know I screwed up, I do. I should have told Nero that Maude was my stepsister, but I was so afraid. I love him, and this was exactly what I thought would happen."

"Did you tell Nero that you love him?" Rapsody asks.

I nod. "Yeah, it just made him angrier."

The bartender slides the shot I ordered in front of me. I nod in thanks and toss it back, wincing at the burn that travels down my chest.

"Just try to be patient," Anabelle says. "I'm sure he'll come around."

Her voice sounds so hopeful that I desperately want to believe her, but every time I blink, Nero's face after he found out haunts my memory. I'm not sure there's any coming back from that.

"Have you guys seen him at all?" I eat all my meals in my bedroom in the west wing and try to be out of the manor as much as possible. At first, I was glad to keep staying there.

But as the days drag on, every corner just feels like a reminder of him.

I need to find my own place sooner than later.

Anabelle and Rapsody share a look. "We tracked him down and tried to talk to him about what's going on with you guys, but he wasn't having it."

I should have expected as much, but the confirmation feels like someone is squeezing my ribs and strangling me to death. I nod slowly and blink back my tears.

Rapsody squeezes my arm, and that's when I notice that she now has a wedding band alongside her engagement ring. I blink a few times. Before she can pull her hand away, I grip her wrist and look more closely.

"What's this?"

She pulls her hand away. "I'm sorry. We thought it was best if we didn't say anything, given what you're going through."

"You and Kol got married?" For the first time since everything between Nero and myself imploded, a genuine smile forms on my face.

She nods, looking as though she's trying to bite back her excitement. "We slipped off to Atlanta and got married at the same city hall we originally intended to be married in. It was just the two of us."

I lean over on my stool and draw her into a hug. "That's amazing. Congratulations! I can't believe you were going to hide it from me."

When I pull away, she shrugs and looks a tad embarrassed. "I just didn't want to make you feel any worse, that's all."

"Ladies, any good news you two have will actually make me feel better. Trust me."

"Okay," Rapsody says.

"Are you going on a honeymoon or anything?" I ask her.

For the next while, we chat about what's going on in Anabelle and Rapsody's lives. It feels good to not be solely focused on how I'm feeling about the end to Nero's and my relationship. I know that as soon as I lie down in my bed tonight, he'll be at the top of my mind again.

"How are things going at the studio?" Anabelle asks.

"I'm almost ready to go. My heart wasn't in it. I just couldn't get motivated to finish everything before the original open date. But I think it's time I just get on with it."

Nero already hates me. The last thing I want is for him to think I'm not going to make good on my promise to pay him back for the money he lent me to renovate the place.

"That sounds like a good idea. It will help get your mind off things," Rapsody says.

"That's what I'm hoping." I give her a weak smile.

Regardless of whether my heart is fully in it, the show must go on, as they say. So I promise myself right then and there that next Saturday will be my grand opening celebration.

I worked my ass off, but I made it happen somehow. Tomorrow morning is the grand opening, and I'm so nervous. It's late Friday night, and I'm just double-checking everything so it's perfect and ready to go for the morning. The decorations are up. I've sent the reminder emails to everyone who expressed interest in coming. I checked with the bakery that my platter of goodies will be ready for me to pick up first thing in the morning. And my playlist is all cued up and ready to go. I have infographics taped up throughout the studio explaining the different types of dance and the benefits of each, and my point-of-sale system is in working order so I can sign people up for classes.

I'm good to go.

With one last look around the space, I turn off the lights and lock the door before I set off down the sidewalk toward my car.

I'm still driving the fancy car Nero bought me, though I wish I could trade it in for my old car. I don't feel right driving it knowing how much he hates me now, but at the moment, I don't have a choice.

For some reason, Magnolia Bend was busy this morning, and I had to park down the road. When my vehicle comes into view, I sigh, happy to be able to go to bed soon. I'm so tired from this week, but I also know that the second I drive past Midnight Manor's iron gates, I'll be flooded with memories and regret.

My hand reaches for the car door, but I'm yanked back. My purse drops to the ground as the smell of alcohol floats to my nostrils.

"You ruined my life, you fucking cunt. Time for me to ruin yours."

I stiffen at the sound of Freddie's voice and wiggle in his hold, struggling to get free, but he's too strong. I fight him as he drags me into a nearby alley.

CHAPTER
THIRTY-THREE

NERO

I head into the dining room for breakfast on Friday morning and almost turn around when I see Sid's the only one in the room.

Great. Just what I'm in the mood for.

But I'm starving, so I enter the room. I sit and dish out my meal without saying a word. We continue like that in awkward silence for at least five minutes before Sid breaks the silence.

"Did you hear the news about Kol and Rapsody?"

I look up from my phone at him. "No. Everything okay?" After everything that went down with those two last year, it's a valid question.

"They flew to Atlanta last week and tied the knot. They're married."

Even though I'm still pissed at Sid, I smile. "Good for them."

A month ago, I thought I might follow in their same footsteps, but no longer.

It's quiet again for a few minutes, during which time I question whether it's even really worth it to still be pissed at Sid given what happened with Cinder. He was probably protecting me and had a better sense than I did of the person she was.

"Asher filled me in on what went down with Cinder."

My hand clenches around my fork. "Don't bother with the told-you-sos."

Though I've moved on from my anger and into grief, I feel a little spark light in my veins, knowing Sid's about to start his shit again.

He holds up his hands in front of him. "I'm not gonna say that. I'm going to say the opposite. I heard about what went down, and yeah, it's shitty she lied to you. No doubt. But I saw you two together. She loved you, kid."

My jaw clenches. "People who love you don't lie to you."

Sid knows why I'm so sensitive about people close to me lying. He was there when I found out the biggest lie of all, and it crushed me as a kid.

"Maybe. Or maybe they do when they think the truth won't change anything, and all it will do is hurt you."

Our gazes lock and hold. Somewhere in there, I think there's an apology and an explanation for what he and my brothers did all those years ago.

"If you really think that I should just forgive Cinder and move on, then why did you say all that shit about her?"

He frowns and shrugs. "I don't know. My head's been a mess lately." He pushes his chair back and stands. "Listen, all I'm saying is that no matter what happened, she loved you. That was obvious to anyone around you two. The question is, do you love her enough to get past this? Because no one is perfect, Nero. We all have our regrets, but just because someone isn't perfect, it doesn't mean they aren't worth loving."

My throat tightens as I watch him leave the room.

I want to forgive her, I do. The question is, can I?

I MANAGED to stay away for a week, when I was still angry. But as the anger gave way to devastation, I found myself once again stalking her, needing to know her every move. Which is why I've been across the street and spying on Cinder through the large front window of her studio for hours.

I can't fight the feeling of pride when I look at all she's accomplished. It's been clear to me the whole time how passionate she is about this endeavor, and to see it complete and ready to open makes me wish we were on better terms so that I could wrap my arms around her and tell her what a good job she's done.

The lights inside the studio flip off. I watch her lock the door and start down the sidewalk toward her vehicle as my phone vibrates in my pocket. I pull it out and see that it's a message from Asher telling me that he's arranged for a celebratory dinner for Kol and Rapsody this Sunday evening, and he expects me to be there. I roll my eyes.

A sound from the road makes me look up.

My heart almost stops.

Cinder is being dragged into the alleyway between buildings as she struggles with whoever is covering her mouth.

Adrenaline fires in my veins, and I exit my car, pocketing my phone and running across the street toward them. Fear burns in my lungs and has my eyes wide as I reach the alley and see Cinder pushed against the side of the building, mouth still covered by some greasy guy's hand as he hovers over her.

This motherfucker is going to wish he was never born.

I race toward them, and the sound of my feet hitting the concrete must alert them to my presence because they both turn in my direction. It's then I recognize the assailant as Lisa's shitty ex, Freddie.

"Get the fuck away from her!" I run toward them.

Freddie keeps one hand on Cinder but shifts to face me, pointing a gun in my direction.

"No!" Cinder screams. She yanks his arm, and the bullet hits the brick wall to my right.

"Fucking bitch," he shouts and turns the gun on her.

"No!" I shout, running toward them.

The gunshot is deafening as I slam into him and tackle him to the ground. He grunts, and I scramble for the gun. I grab the hand holding the gun and slam it against the ground, then shove my arm down on his neck between his chin and sternum, pressing as hard as I can. He bucks, but I hold tight, continuing to slam his hand down on the pavement until it dislodges the gun. He's passed out. Or maybe dead. I don't care.

Crawling forward, I palm the gun, then take out the magazine and bullet from the chamber. I stand to go to Cinder, and my blood runs cold as I watch blood pour from her side.

"No, no, no, no!" I rush over and set the gun on the ground, kneeling beside her.

The sound of sirens ring through the night. Obviously, someone must've heard the gunshots and called the police.

Quickly pulling off my shirt, I ball it up and use it to put pressure on her wound, hoping to slow the bleeding.

"Why did you have to do that, princess? I'd rather it be me than you." Tears track down my cheeks. I shake my head, thinking of how I've treated her these past couple of weeks and wishing I could take it back. "Don't you dare die, Cinder, do you hear me? Don't you dare die!"

Despite me pushing down hard on the wound, my shirt soaks with blood.

"Step away from the gun!"

I look over my shoulder and see the police with guns drawn and a paramedic with a bag waiting behind them.

I raise my hands and step away. "Please help her!"

One of the cops comes forward and pushes me up against the wall, yanking my hands behind me and cuffing me. When he turns me around to pat me down, Cinder is already being cared for by the paramedic. Thank God.

"What the hell happened here?" the cop asks.

I ignore him and call out to the paramedic, "Is she going to be okay?" *Please tell me she's going to survive.*

"We're going to do our best, sir," he says.

"I've got a pulse on this one," the female paramedic helping Freddie says.

"We need to transport her to hospital ASAP. I'm calling the helicopter," the guy says and presses the button on his radio.

"Hey, I asked you a question," the cop says again.

"I need to go with her when they transport her."

"You're not going anywhere, son." He tries to lead me down the alleyway, but I put up a fight, not wanting to be away from Cinder. The cop shoves me into the wall. "Resisting arrest is only going to make this worse for you."

"I'm not leaving her!" I hate using my family name like this, but it's for Cinder, so I have no shame. "My name is Nero Voss, and that man assaulted and shot my girlfriend."

The word girlfriend slips out without a thought. But it feels right. Because I know now that if she survives this, I will never let her go again. Ever.

"Voss? Like the Vosses that live at the top of the hill?"

"One and the same. Check my wallet for my ID if you want."

He reaches out his hand to his partner for the wallet he took out when he did his initial pat down and flips open my wallet to my ID.

"Listen, I'll answer anything you want me to, but I need to make sure she's all right first. I need to be on that helicopter with her."

"Sir, there's no room for you on the helicopter," the male paramedic says. "You'd be compromising the level of care we can give her. You'll have to meet us there."

I clench my teeth—hard—wanting to argue with him, but I don't want to make it harder for them to save her life.

"Fine. Whatever." I look back at the cop. "Just take these cuffs off, and I promise once I know she's going to be okay, I'll tell you whatever you want to know."

The cop talking to me looks at his partner, who nods. Clearly his buddy knows that my family has the ability to make their lives a living hell. They'll be stuck at a desk job for the rest of their careers if they don't fall in line.

The cop pulls out the key to undo the handcuffs just as they're moving Cinder onto a stretcher. "I'm sorry about this, Mr. Voss. We didn't realize who you were when we arrived."

"It's fine." I rush over to the stretcher and notice that Freddie is gaining consciousness. I get the cops' attention. "He's the one who shot her. That's who you should have cuffs on."

The sound of a helicopter fills the night as the paramedic pushes the stretcher down the alley toward the road. They'll have to go to the open field just past downtown for the helicopter to land safely.

I bend down and kiss Cinder's forehead. "Hang in there, princess. I'll meet you there."

Then I run the rest of the way to my car, desperate to reunite with her and beg her to forgive me for being a complete asshole.

CHAPTER
THIRTY-FOUR

CINDER

I walk through the mist, not knowing which way to go. It's all so confusing. Every other time I felt as though I was being pulled forward, and I had that voice to guide me. But now I just feel lost in an abyss.

Walking in one direction, I turn around and start in another. The fog never disperses or lessens, and I circle around, more confused than ever.

Then there's a voice in my head. "We're losing her!"

"I need another clamp—"

The words fade away, and the fog recedes. But the more the fog lifts, all I see is darkness surrounding me.

"Cinder."

It's that same voice I heard in my dreams at Midnight Manor.

"Cinder..."

I turn toward the voice.

"You have to come this way." The voice is kind, and I step in that direction.

As I move, the fog descends again and thickens.

"That's it. Keep coming, Cinder. Keep walking."

I do, but then there's a flash of light. Then nothing.

THE FIRST THING I notice is constant beeping and the smell of antiseptic. I want to open my eyes, but they're so heavy, and I'm tired.

"Why isn't she waking up?"

Nero? It sounds like him, but it's muffled.

"She will. Her body needs rest. It's healing."

Anabelle.

Warmth tightens around my hand. I squeeze.

"Holy shit! She just squeezed my hand," I hear Nero's voice again. "Princess, can you hear me? Can you squeeze my hand again?"

I squeeze as hard as I can, using every ounce of willpower in me.

"I'll go get the doctor," Anabelle says, and I hear what sounds like a squeaky door.

"Can you open your eyes? Even just a little? Please, Cinder, I've been so scared."

It's the fear in his voice that has me trying hard to open my eyes. It takes a few attempts, and when I get them open just a sliver, the lights sear my eyes. I slam my eyes shut again.

"That's great! That's great! Now see if you can do it a little more." He squeezes my hand.

I try again, and this time, I get them open slowly. Nero's standing beside the bed, looking down at me with tears in his eyes.

"Oh, thank God." He presses his forehead to mine and wetness coats my cheek, but it isn't my own.

"I need you to back up, Mr. Voss," a deep voice from behind him says.

A man in a white lab coat looks over me from the other side of the bed. It's a bit of a blur. He asks me questions about how I'm feeling and whether I'm in pain. It's as if as soon as he mentions it, my brain takes notice of the throbbing pain on my left side. He goes on to explain to me that I had surgery to repair a gunshot wound in my side.

"You were very lucky it didn't hit any internal organs. It will take some time to recover, but you should be fine with no lasting repercussions down the road."

I don't say anything. I'm so confused. I don't remember how I even got here.

Once the doctor leaves, I turn my attention to Nero. "What happened? Who shot me?"

I try to remember, but everything is a blur. I remember leaving the dance studio and being glad to be able to go to bed soon because I was so tired. And I remember thinking that I was going to feel sad when I drove past the gates... because Nero wasn't speaking to me anymore.

Everything comes back to me in a rush—Maude and Louise showing up at the studio, Nero being upset with me, and us breaking up. So why is he here?

"Go on and tell her, Nero. I'm going to give you guys some privacy." I hadn't even realized that Anabelle returned.

"What are you doing here?" I ask once she's gone.

"Of course I'm here." He grips my hand tighter.

"The last thing I remember was that you still hated me. Did we make up, and I just forgot?"

He shakes his head, frowning. "No, but we're going to. Because I'm never letting you go again, Cinder. But we'll save that conversation for when you're healed."

"Okay." The only reason I agree is because I don't have any energy. I'm so tired. "Who shot me then?"

His jaw clenches. "Freddie did. He ambushed you after you left the studio. I tried to intervene, and he aimed the gun at me. You saved my life."

"I did?"

He presses his lips together and nods. "Yeah. Even though we weren't together, you still saved my life, and you got shot as a result, almost ending your own." He shakes his head as if he can't believe it, and his eyes water. "Don't take a bullet for me ever again, you hear me?"

I'm not surprised by what he tells me. Except the part about Freddie ambushing me. There's no way I would stand by and do nothing if Nero's life was in jeopardy.

"What happened to Freddie?" I ask.

"I tell you all that, and you want to know what happened to Freddie? Cinder, you saved my life and almost died in the process. I was so scared when I saw you lying there, bleeding. I thought the universe was stealing someone else I love from me."

My eyes widen when he mentions the word love, but my eyelids get heavier and heavier. I don't have long until my body demands that I rest. "So what happened with Freddie?"

I need to know that he's not a threat to me or Nero or Lisa and her kids.

"He's been arrested and charged with attempted murder, among other things."

"Good. That's good." But before I can say anything else, my eyelids close, and I drift off.

CHAPTER
THIRTY-FIVE

CINDER

A week passes before I'm allowed to leave the hospital, though a nurse will come see me at the manor every day to ensure that I'm progressing well. The next week will be spent mostly in bed, except for the daily exercises they want me to do. That just consists of getting out of bed and walking ten or twenty feet. It still hurts when I move, and Nero insists on putting me in a wheelchair and pushing me when we arrive at Midnight Manor.

He's been by my side the entire week, only leaving the hospital in search of food or a shower and always promptly returning. We haven't discussed the breakup or what it means that he's stayed with me and mentioned love. It seems like an unspoken agreement that we won't broach the subject until life has returned somewhat to normal.

But I'm tired of waiting. In many ways, the not knowing feels worse than knowing he may have forgiven me, but he

325

still doesn't want to be with me. Maybe he was just freaked out when I almost died, and with every day that passes, he realizes that his feelings aren't as strong as he thought they were.

He pushes the wheelchair into my room first, not his, and my heart sinks. I'll sleep alone, and I'm back where I started when I moved here—in my own room.

I try not to let my disappointment show. He's already done so much more for me than he had to, and I'm grateful. I'm not going to guilt him into wanting to be with me.

He helps me up from the wheelchair, and I wince.

"You okay?" he asks.

I nod. "Yeah. Just give me a sec." I take a few deep breaths and nod that I'm good to get into the bed. He helps me get in, then stuffs pillows behind me so I'm sitting up on an angle. "Thank you."

He meets my gaze. "Of course." He stands awkwardly, shifting his weight. "Guess I'll let you get some rest. You must be tired and sore from the trip home. I'll put your phone on the bedside table." He pulls it out of his pocket and sets it down. "If you need anything, just text or call me, okay?"

I press my lips together and nod, trying to keep the words in my mouth that want to spill like jelly beans out of a jar.

He nods and turns to leave the room.

But as soon as he's crossed the threshold, I call out for him. "Nero. Wait!"

He must hear something in my voice because he turns right around and rushes back to the bed. "What's wrong?" His eyes skate over me from head to toe, assessing.

"I need to know what's going on with us. This limbo stuff is killing me."

His shoulders sag. "I think you should heal some more before we have this conversation."

There it is. We're not getting back together.

"Because I'm not going to like the outcome?" My eyebrows raise.

"Because the most important thing is that you get better. That should be your focus."

I shake my head before he's done speaking. "No. I'll get better whether we have this conversation or not. I need to know if you forgive me."

He sits on the side of the bed and takes my hand. "I do forgive you. I do. And I have my own apology to make. I shouldn't have reacted the way I did. Yes, I had a right to be upset, but to completely cut you off like that and not consider how you were feeling wasn't right. But for you to understand why I reacted the way I did, there's something I have to tell you."

He makes it sound ominous, and I brace myself for whatever he's about to say. My stomach bubbles with nerves. "Okay..."

Nero sighs and pushes his free hand through his hair. "I found out something when I was younger. The day my dad died actually. Something that everyone in my family had been keeping from me my entire life."

I squeeze his hand. "What was it?"

"Ramsey Voss was not my biological father."

I gasp, and my free hand flies up to my mouth. "He wasn't?"

He shakes his head. "No. Apparently my biological father was the man my mother had a long-time affair with. The one who killed her."

"Oh, Nero." I squeeze his hand harder, wishing I could sit up and pull him to me. "How did you find out?"

"My father—the only one I ever knew anyway—threw it in my face that day as a barb. Apparently, my brothers knew the whole time and had tried to protect me from it. They were always trying to protect me. But Ramsey was cruel and liked nothing more than to inflict pain, both physical and emotional, so he used that knowledge to hurt me. Knowing him, he was probably salivating for years, waiting until the truth would have its greatest impact."

"How did you feel when you found out?"

"At first, I was angry at my brothers for hiding the truth from me. I was angry with my mom, too, though that feeling was more complicated because she had already passed away. Eventually, I realized it didn't make a difference who my biological father was. Both he and the father who had raised me were dead, as was my mother. And my brothers never treated me any differently than they treat each other. It's not like I think I could've lived a better life had I known earlier and spent time with my real dad. He murdered my mom. He wasn't a good person either."

"I'm sorry you had to find out that way."

He nods. "You can probably understand why I don't like surprises based on lies. It takes me back, dredges all that shit up again." He frowns. "So when I found out that you'd lied and kept from me who Maude was to you..." He squeezes the bridge of his nose then meets my gaze. "I should have let you explain, been more understanding."

I shake my head. "No, you had every right to be upset with me."

"I know, I know. But I just cut you off at the knees. Ended things. Wouldn't hear you out or even speak to you, and that wasn't right. I'm sorry." His gaze is full of remorse, and I attempt to touch his cheek but cringe when a sharp pain pierces my side.

"Thank you for telling me. I understand better now why you reacted the way you did."

"If I could take it back, I would. In a second." He brings the hand he's holding up to his lips and kisses my knuckles.

"I have to apologize too."

He shakes his head as if he's not going to let me.

"No, Nero. Let me say this."

With a deep sigh, he nods.

"I was wrong for not telling you that Maude was my step-sister. The moment I knew I was falling for you, I should have come clean. Even if I was scared. Even if I thought you might end our relationship because of it. I should have trusted that what we had would be strong enough to survive."

329

He leans forward and places a chaste kiss on my lips. "You're forgiven, princess."

The weight of the world lifts off my shoulders, and tears pool in the corners of my eyes in relief.

"I'm still so pissed at myself that it took you almost dying for me to come to my senses. When I saw you bleeding..." He squeezes his eyes shut. "I've never been more terrified in my life. The idea of you no longer being on this earth was unfathomable. I don't know how I would have been able to go on."

His words remind me of something I've been wondering about. "How did you know Freddie had ambushed me?"

Embarrassment colors his cheeks for a beat, and he glances down at the comforter. "I was still watching you. I swear, Cinder, when I saw him with his fucking hands on you, I thought I was going to have a heart attack and keel over. I have never felt more desperate than that night."

"You were watching me?" I ask softly. I'd assumed all of that had stopped after the night Louise and Maude confronted me.

"Yeah." His voice is rough. "I was able to stop for about a week, then I couldn't stand it anymore. Even though I was still processing it all, I needed to have my eyes on you."

"Thank you for saving me," I whisper, not wanting to imagine what the alternative would have been if he hadn't shown up.

"Princess, you're the one who saved me. In more ways than one." He rests his forehead against mine. When he pulls away, he looks in my eyes with conviction. "I love you. More than I've ever loved anyone else in my life. I need you with me forever, and I refuse to let anything, or anyone, ever tear us apart again. You have my commitment that I will love you until the end of my days with all that I have. My life means nothing if I don't have you in it. I haven't felt unconditional love like this since I was a child from my mom. Thank you for loving me the way you do."

A tear races down my cheek. Nero loves me. My eyes drift closed for a beat because I never thought I'd hear those words from him. Thought I'd ruined my chance to ever hear them.

I know exactly what he means, though. I'm an orphan too, and if you're not one, it's hard to understand how much you crave being loved again once you've lost it.

"I love you too. So much."

He kisses me gently then pulls away. "Don't ever leave me."

I shake my head. "Never."

"I'll never leave you," he says.

And though they're not wedding vows, they're a vow just the same. One we both intend to keep.

EPILOGUE

Two weeks have passed since Cinder returned to Midnight Manor, and she's doing a lot better. She still has to take it easy, which is driving her crazy.

I had to convince her that it's still too early to open up the dance school, that she needs to keep resting and healing so she can be at her best once it does open. Besides, the doctor told her she still can't dance, so as much as she hates it, she's had to be somewhat sedentary except for the walks we take around the property.

She won't admit it, but they take a lot out of her. She almost always naps after.

I'm running out of things to keep her entertained around the manor, so today I decided to pull out some old home movies for us to watch in the theater room. I figure she might get a kick out of seeing my brothers and me when we were younger.

I don't have to worry about dredging up the past because my dad isn't in these movies. These are the ones my mom filmed with just us boys. It's been over a decade since I've looked at them, so I'm not entirely sure how I'll feel viewing them.

The last time I watched them, they made me feel sad for all I'd lost. But I have so much to look forward to in my life now that I have a different perspective. I'll always miss my mom and wish I could have gotten to know her better, but I feel confident that she'd be happy with where my life is today.

I've just cued up the first movie, and I take a seat beside Cinder.

"This was a great idea." She grins. "I can't wait to see what you all looked like when you were little. Was Sid as moody then as he is now? Was Asher always the leader?"

I chuckle. "I guess neither of them has changed that much."

"And what about you?" She takes the bag of M&M's she brought in and dumps them into the bowl of popcorn in her lap.

I cringe. "I don't know how you eat that."

She playfully rolls her eyes. "I told you, don't knock it until you try it. You'd be surprised how yummy it is." Cinder holds the bowl out to me, and I hold up my hand, shaking my head.

"I'm good."

She shrugs and turns her attention to the screen. "Okay, let's get started."

334

I hit Play on the remote.

"Is that the pond we walked by?" Cinder asks.

"That's the one." I chuckle when Kol pops on the screen. I'd guess he's about eight or nine. "That's Kol."

He races down the dock and jumps, pulling his knees to his chest and shouting "Cannonball!"

Female laughter from behind the camera fills the theater. My mom's laugh. I'd forgotten what a good laugh she had. Over the years, it's faded from memory, but hearing it now, it's all too familiar, and my chest is hit with a pang of nostalgia.

Next Asher comes on screen and does a perfect dive off the end of the dock.

"Let me guess, that was Asher?" Cinder says.

I turn to look at her. "How'd you know?"

She shrugs. "I'm not sure actually. Just seems like such an Asher thing to do."

We both laugh and look back at the screen.

Oh god. I forgot about this.

Sid is pulling me down the dock by the arm, and five-year-old me is trying my best not to go with him. I was terrified to jump in, even with a life jacket on.

Cinder's hands fly up to her face. "Oh my gosh! Is that little guy you?"

"Yup. I wasn't a strong swimmer, and I remember how scared I was. I'd never jumped in before."

"C'mon, Nero. Don't be a baby," Sid says in the video.

Asher and Kol are treading water, trying to encourage me to jump. But I'm not having it. I'm doing my best to stop Sid from dragging me to the edge, but he was bigger and older than me, so I didn't stand much of a chance.

"Obsidian, leave him alone if he doesn't want to go in," my mom says.

The sound of her voice pushes the air from my lungs. It's been so long since I've heard it. But rather than feel sorrowful, I'm glad I still have the opportunity to revisit it when I want. I won't wait so long to pull these tapes out again.

"Was that your mom?" Cinder asks.

Something in her tone has me turning to face her. All the color has drained from her face, and her mouth hangs open as she looks at the screen.

I hit Pause on the video. "Princess, what's wrong?"

"Nero, was that your mom?" She turns and looks at me with an urgency to her voice.

"Yeah... why?"

"I know that voice."

My forehead wrinkles. "How could you know that voice?"

Her eyes widen. "The night you found me at the basement door... the night I found you in the aviary... the night I was shot..." She swallows hard.

My chest tightens. She's worrying me now. I have no idea what the hell is going on.

"I thought I was sleepwalking all those times. There was this mist I couldn't see through, but there was a voice beckoning me forward, saying my name over and over again. Nero, that was the voice. It was your mom's voice!"

"Are you sure?"

She nods frantically. "Absolutely. I'm telling you it was her." Tears gather in her eyes. "Nero, what do you think that means?"

A swell of emotion fills my chest, and I struggle for a breath. "I think it means my mom knew before I did how right you were for me." I cup her face, kissing her gently.

When I pull away, her eyes are full of tears. "I wish I could have met her."

I lower my forehead to hers. "I do too."

We sit like that for a few minutes, breathing each other in. I don't always feel close to my deceased mother when I think of her, since I was so young when she passed away, but between the videos we're watching and what Cinder has just revealed, I swear I feel her spirit here with us.

I sigh and pull away. "Should we watch some more?"

"Of course. I want to know her as best I can."

Smiling, I give Cinder a quick kiss then shove my hand in the bowl with the popcorn and M&M's mix. Then I toss some in my mouth.

"Well?" Her eyebrows rise.

I chew, rocking my head side to side. "Not bad. Better than I thought."

With a smile, she rests her head on my shoulder. I click Play and the video starts up again.

The longer we watch the videos, the more a feeling of peace comes over me. I may have lost the love of my mother, but she helped me gain the love of the most amazing woman.

The door to the theater room opens, and I straighten up and look over my shoulder. Kol stands at the entrance, hands in his pockets, staring at the screen. I hit Pause.

"Jesus. I haven't seen these in... shit, I don't know how long," he says, not letting his eyes stray from the screen.

"We're taking a trip down memory lane."

"Did you come across the one where Mom tried to make macarons?" He chuckles, and I smile.

"Oh yeah. Cinder and I were laughing over how Mom didn't believe smoke was coming out of the oven when you first told her. Remember how disappointed she was that they didn't turn out?"

"And then she placed an order for some from that fancy bakery in New York." A sad smile crosses his face.

We're all quiet, and Cinder takes my hand.

"What's up? I know you're not just here to see what we're up to," I say.

Kol sighs, shoves his hands in his pockets, and walks over to us. "Sid's disappeared."

I frown. "What do you mean he's disappeared?"

"No one knows where he is. He's been gone for two weeks,

and we're not sure if he's just laying low or if something happened."

I think back to the last time I saw him... it would have been the day Cinder was attacked. I hadn't thought much of not seeing him lately. I've been giving all my attention to Cinder since she's been back, and before that, I was at the hospital twenty-four-seven. We've been eating all our meals together in different places in the house, and if we were in the dining room and Sid wasn't there, that wasn't unusual. He travels for work sometimes.

"You have no idea where he is?"

Kol shakes his head. "He hasn't used his credit cards, his phone, or logged into Voss Enterprises at all. It's like he's vanished."

"What about the plane?" Cinder asks.

Kol moves his attention to her. "No flight plans. If he flew somewhere, he didn't use one of our planes."

She bites her bottom lip and looks at me.

I think back to our last conversation and the way he's been acting, how he said his head was a mess. I took the comment about not everyone being perfect as him talking about Cinder, but what if he was talking about himself?

"You don't think he'd hurt himself, do you?" I ask Kol.

The two of them are usually thick as thieves, but with Rapsody in Kol's life, I bet that's no longer the case.

Kol stiffens, and his forehead wrinkles. "Why would you ask that?"

I relay my last conversation with Sid to him.

"Fuck." He runs his palm over the top of his head.

We're all quiet, thinking of the possibilities.

I don't know what Sid is up to. All I know is that my brother better be okay.

The End

Don't miss the next book in our Midnight Manor series, Twisted Truths.

ACKNOWLEDGMENTS

Once again, welcome back to Midnight Manor!

When we first started planning out the series, Nero's book was going to be the second one in the series. That's until we got halfway through writing MOONLIT THORNS and realized that we needed a little extra time to let Nero's relationship with Maude fizzle out. So, we put him on ice until it was his turn.

From the moment he hit the page, Nero wasn't quite as big of an asshole as his brothers. There's no other way to say it than that. LOL But that didn't mean he wasn't hiding things, as you now know. Nero had the potential to veer down a dangerous path with his stalking tendencies and was always trying to toe the line so things didn't go too far. It was fun discovering who he was as we wrote this one.

The biggest stumbling block when we began writing this book was figuring out how to incorporate the fairy tale retelling aspect of the Cinderella story into Midnight Whispers. When we set out to write this series, we didn't want to write carbon copies of the fairy tales themselves, but rather stories inspired by the original tales. Hence why, in our story, Cinder and Nero meet at the ball in the very first chapter of the book, but we still don't have Nero discover who Cinder really is until closer to the end.

A big part of the fun of writing these later books in the series is seeing snippets of where the other brothers are in their lives with the women they love, so we hope you're enjoying the cameos, too!

We have to give much thanks to everyone who helped bring this book to market...

A big shout to Regina Wamba for the gorgeous cover. Her work on the entire Midnight Manor series is breathtaking.

Thanks as always to Cassie at Joy editing for the line edits and for My Brother's Editor for the proofreading. You both helped make this story what it is today.

The Valentine PR crew always keeps us in check and follows up to make sure we're hitting those deadlines. Not only do we need it, but we appreciate it!

A HUGE hug to every blogger, influencer and reader who continues to support this series! We genuinely appreciate every review, edit, recommendation to your reader friends, rating, and social media shout-out you give us. We see you and are so, so grateful! <3

And of course, a massive thanks to YOU for picking this story and making it all the way to the end. We appreciate you spending your precious time in the world of Midnight Manor.

Well, there's only one brother left to find his HEA and he might be the most tortured. Obsidian was aptly named despite the polished veneer he presents to the world. He's slowly been unraveling book after book, and we suppose it's time for us to put him back together. It's going to take a strong woman to be able to take him on.

Make sure you pick up TWISTED TRUTHS, our reimagining of The Little Mermaid, to see how it all unfolds!

xo,

Piper & Rayne

ABOUT P. RAYNE

P. Rayne is the pseudonym for the darker side of the USA Today Bestselling Author duo, Piper Rayne. Under P. Rayne you'll find dark, forbidden and sexy romances.

ALSO BY P. RAYNE

Midnight Manor

Moonlit Thorns

Shattered Vows

Midnight Whispers

Twisted Truths

Mafia Academy

Vow of Revenge

Corrupting the Innocent

Corrupting the Mafia King's Sister

Craving My Rival

Standalones

Beautifully Scarred

Made in United States
Orlando, FL
02 September 2024

51066024R00214